A
Murder
in Old Town

A Murder in Old Town

A NOVEL

KAY CORDTZ

SUNSTONE PRESS
SANTA FE

Note: Quotes from "Old Town Road" lyrics are by Lil Nas X.

Sunstone books may be purchased for educational, business, or sales promotional use.
For information please write: Special Markets Department, Sunstone Press,
P.O. Box 2321, Santa Fe, New Mexico 87504-2321.
Printed on acid-free paper

Library of Congress Cataloging-in-Publication Data

Names: Cordtz, Kay, 1950- author.
Title: A murder in Old Town : a novel / Kay Cordtz.
Description: Santa Fe : Sunstone Press, [2024] | Includes readers' guide. |
   Summary: "A grandmother from rural New Mexico tries to save her at-risk
   grandson and is herself swept up in a series of criminal acts in today's
   Old Town Albuquerque"-- Provided by publisher.
Identifiers: LCCN 2024022197 | ISBN 9781632936783 (paperback) | ISBN
   9781611397468 (epub)
Subjects: LCGFT: Detective and mystery fiction. | Novels.
Classification: LCC PS3603.O73426 M87 2024 | DDC 813/.6--dc23/eng/20240520

LC record available at https://lccn.loc.gov/2024022197

WWW.SUNSTONEPRESS.COM
SUNSTONE PRESS / POST OFFICE BOX 2321 / SANTA FE, NM 87504-2321 /USA
(505) 988-4418

For Mom and Dad, who taught me to love books

Preface

Albuquerque's Old Town has been continuously inhabited for more than three hundred years. At its core, the Plaza and immediately adjacent streets with their tourist-friendly shops are well protected by private security. But thanks in large part to the intersection of two interstate highways here, the streets outside of those blocks contain all the ills of any big city magnified: homelessness, drugs and sex abuse. Living in Old Town while writing this book, I witnessed many of these dynamics up close and later, during the Covid lockdown, from my balcony. I had little or no contact with my neighbors or others who might have supplied details about incidents not covered on the local news.

But criminal activity in the neighborhood and a strange series of coincidences led me to begin wondering and imagining how all these events might be related. As Eudora Welty advised, "Write what you don't know about what you know." So I let my imagination connect the dots. My main character, Fortuna, is physically based on a homeless woman I used to see on the bridge and later on a bench in Old Town. While I don't know anything about that woman, she reminded me that every homeless person has a story.

In my view, the juxtaposition of this historic place where people struggled to survive with the culture of 21st century hedonism blooming all around it was particularly striking. I lived for decades in northern New Mexico, where the codes and values of the people in the north, particularly the elderly, are not unknown to me. They are among the wisest and most hardworking people I have known. But I also watched a young generation lost to alcohol and drug addiction while their parents and grandparents struggled to find a way to save their children.

Nearby, career-focused parents from Los Alamos are oblivious to what their good students are doing until it's too late. This book is, to some degree, a cautionary tale.

—Kay Cordtz

F

Fortuna

Fortuna was sitting at her usual place on the bridge when the boy ran into the river. The Rio Grande was muddy, running low. Sandbars of various sizes had appeared, some already covered with weeds. The boy was able to splash his way across, tripping over underwater debris and falling once, his dripping t-shirt clinging to his thin frame. It was a hot June day in Albuquerque and Fortuna had been dozing over a book, too stupefied by the heat to concentrate. When the boy fell, the river current moved him into her line of sight. When he turned to look behind, she had a brief but clear glimpse of his terrified face before he ran into the bosque on the far side.

"Ay abuela, just like Billy and his cousins," she said, continuing an ongoing dialogue with her dead grandmother, Ofelia. "Young men play so rough. Then they will grow up to beat up their wives...break their arms. Like Diego did." She rubbed her left arm as she surveyed the cottonwood and coyote willow forest on the east bank of the river, leaves shivering in the occasional breeze. "Whoever he is running from will be along any minute."

Earlier in the morning Fortuna had walked down to the riverbank to wash up. She had removed her light jacket and her shoes and stockings and waded in until the water nearly touched the hem of her dress. The muddy water was cool and she used her good hand to splash some on her face and neck.

"Mira abuela, my arms have these big black spots! Remember when I wore sleeveless dresses to church? I know there was gossip about me, that I was vain and disrespectful. But really I was just young and proud."

She unzipped the rolling suitcase that accompanied her everywhere and retrieved a small towel to dry her feet and legs before putting on her shoes and stockings. She sat down on a nearby rock to do this, then buried her face in the towel. "I must not cry," she said. "If I start I might not be able to stop." She stood up slowly, retrieved her hat from a nearby tree stump, placed it securely on her head and pulled her suitcase up the path to her perch on the bridge.

Things were usually so quiet on the bench. It sat in a cutout where a curve of chain link fencing replaced the solid wall and offered a perfect river view. For months, she had been staying here until dusk, watching the birds and dreaming of the mastodons and sabertoothed cats that had roamed the Rio Grande Valley a hundred thousand years ago, when the river was part of the ocean. In the process, she had become expert at ignoring all human activity. Occasionally, a pedestrian or two would cross the sidewalk behind her but Albuquerque is not a walking town, except for its poorest citizens. Cars could not stop on the bridge without obstructing traffic and there was no bus stop nearby.

She became aware of some shouting and honking and an ambulance scream farther east up Central Avenue. But the umbrella that protected her from the midday sun also blocked her view of what might be happening outside of it. Now, sirens were approaching the bridge, followed by flashing red and blue lights shimmering in the heat. Fortuna was aware of the police activity but during her six months in the city she had seen too much police overreaction to pay it much mind. To see down the road would mean repositioning the umbrella and her one functional hand had fallen asleep. If she had looked, she would have seen the roadblock being set up across the entrance to the bridge and would have been aware of the squad car slowing alongside the curb behind her. A car door slammed, but Fortuna still did not turn, hoping in vain to avoid conversation.

Two APD officers hustled around the umbrella into her line of sight, a big, middle-aged Anglo and a young one, light-skinned. Either Hispano or Indio, she thought. Maybe both.

"Lady, what did you see? Did you see anyone?" The big cop was apparently too agitated to be appropriately respectful to a woman of her age, Fortuna thought. And so loud. Who did he think he was addressing? But she shook out her tingling hand, moved the umbrella and looked up.

"Abuela, por favor, que ha visto?" The young officer seemed to sense that she required a more polite address to feel like being helpful.

But the older cop exploded at his partner's deference. "C'mon lady, it's an emergency! Did you see him? Where did he go?" He gestured towards the river.

As awareness dawned that they were asking about the young man who ran into the river, Fortuna pointed toward where he had turned around and looked at her.

"Why are you chasing him?" Fortuna asked. Neither one answered. She replayed the event in her mind, but its edges were hazy. Most of her life had a dreamlike quality since she came to Albuquerque. Did he look directly at her before disappearing into the Bosque? She hadn't tried hard enough to recall the details to be sure, but she thought he met her gaze.

"Did you see him? Will you talk to an officer who can draw a picture of his face?"

Fortuna had never known involvement in a crime investigation to lead to a good outcome. Not even in books.

"I only saw his back," she said. "He was wearing a black t-shirt."

Now she could hear a helicopter coming from the east. As it hovered over the river just beyond the bridge, conversation became impossible.

"You're going to have to leave this area," the young cop said. "Give your name and contact information to the officer at the roadblock."

He waited while Fortuna closed her umbrella and placed her book in the suitcase. She lashed the umbrella to its side. Placing her hat on her head, she stood up to her full six-foot height. The young cop stepped back to allow her to pass. She headed for the roadblock, pulling the suitcase with a dignity that suggested an eccentric socialite more than a homeless waif.

"What's in that suitcase she's hauling around? Takes all kinds," said the old cop.

Since the police had blocked the bridge at both ends, no cars passed and she felt the weight of the eyes of the officers. Her useless left arm hung at her side but the low wall and the swaying trees leading down to the river shielded it from view. As she approached the riverbank, where she had bathed just a few hours before, she saw several officers surrounding a black bicycle lying in the shallow water. The scene beyond the roadblock was chaotic, as cars and buses tried to make U-turns amid honking, shouted curses and other signs of growing road rage. A crowd of bystanders was also gathering. As she came to the end of the sidewalk, an officer listening to his car radio gestured for her to stop.

"We're going to need some information from you," he said. Fortuna gave him her cousin Tina's name instead of her own and repeated what she told the other cops. She said she lived at St. Bridget's Homeless Shelter, where she actually had stayed some months back. The officer wrote it down and allowed her to pass through the roadblock and continue east along Central Avenue, where she was ambushed by a breathless woman in a business suit holding a microphone in front of her face.

"Are you a witness, ma'am?"

"No hablo ingles," Fortuna replied, hurrying away.

The reporter turned to signal to her cameraman, who spoke Spanish, but Fortuna and her suitcase had disappeared into the crowd.

The next day, Fortuna woke with the sun, sitting on her suitcase with her back pressed against the Black Willow tree at the eastern edge of the Old Town park.. She had been fortunate to find no one there when she arrived at dusk, having spent the afternoon reading in the sculpture garden of the Albuquerque Museum. The only place to sit there was a picnic table with no shade. Except for the handful of statues, there was nothing much to look at but it was another place where she could usually be alone. A book as always helped her to while away the hours.

As the sun began to descend, a security guard came to lock up.

"Con permiso," he said respectfully. "I will have to lock the gates. I will unlock them at nine tomorrow morning."

"He must have an abuela too," she whispered. She rose and walked slowly to the Plaza to wait for the sun to go down when it would be dark enough to find a safe place to sleep.

Walking through the park, she saw there was no one camped under the big tree.

"Que buena suerte," she said to Ofelia. "This is the best place to sleep in the park."

On a moonless night like this one, up tight against the massive trunk, she was not liable to be seen and rousted by a cop. Sleeping in the park was forbidden, but it was quiet and free and she was well-practiced at being unobtrusive. Her lame arm was stiff this morning, but she pushed herself up to standing, supported by the tree. She stretched her legs, repositioned her clothing and hat, gathered her belongings and headed back to the bridge, less than a mile down the road.

"It was strange, what happened there yesterday," she said to Ofelia. "I saw that boy's face in a dream last night, but he was running in the fields by our house up north. Or maybe it was someone else." She struggled to recall details but they had vanished, as dreams will. There was something familiar about the boy's face, but she had no friends or acquaintances in Albuquerque so her mind struggled to recall where she might have seen him before. The suffocating Albuquerque heat was rising. It would be good to get to her bench, set up her umbrella, look far away to the north and appreciate the peace of nature without humans.

But as she passed the big family restaurant on Central Avenue, she could see that the roadblock was still in place. A solid line of cars, most with their red lights flashing, was causing another traffic tie-up as officers directed cranky motorists to go back the way they came.

She was more irritated than curious.

"Que chinga," she muttered. "I guess today will not be so lucky." The north-facing bench was her spot; whatever was happening down there, it was disrupting her established routine. She would have to think about where else to go for the day. She headed to a coffee shop in a strip mall nearby where she would sometimes stop for a cup of coffee and a donut in the mornings. Fortuna left her suitcase behind a booth so she would be able to carry her Styrofoam cup and donut in a bag in one hand. On her way back to the booth, she saw a newspaper left on a table. She retrieved it after setting down the coffee. She sat down and spread the front page of the Albuquerque Journal across the table.

A banner headline, Homicide suspect not found after all-day bosque manhunt, dominated a series of photos of the roadblock.

"Albuquerque Police Department homicide detectives are still searching for a man suspected of fatally shooting a man in front of a coffee shop on Central downtown Wednesday morning."

"So that's why they were chasing that boy," she said. "A murder, abuela."

Fortuna scanned to the end of the story. It said the suspect was armed, dressed in black, and officers lost him in the Bosque. The manhunt was to continue all day.

"Ay Dios, the cops will be looking for me. I can't get involved in this, Diego will find me and break my other arm."

She had not seen a gun but this morning, thanks to the dream, she could remember every detail of the boy's face. She had spent too much time and effort covering her tracks to be discovered now. She finished her coffee and stuffed the newspaper into the pocket of her suitcase. She slipped out the backdoor and across the strip mall parking lot leading to a path used by residents of the trailer park behind it. A second-hand store focused on clothing and books was on the corner. She went in and scanned the room until she spotted a plain black umbrella leaning against the wall behind a pile of shoes. Fortuna picked it up and marched to the elderly saleswoman sitting behind a desk at the front of the store.

She brandished the rainbow umbrella that she had found in a dumpster her first week in Albuquerque.

"Can I trade this for the black one?"

The saleswoman looked surprised but recognized a good trade.

"Sure. But it's a pretty uneven trade. Is there anything else you'd like?"

Fortuna crossed the room to replace the black umbrella with her colorful one. Some days, the rainbow umbrella was the only sight that made her smile, but she couldn't allow herself to get nostalgic. It had to be done. She passed a bookshelf filled with worn paperbacks and one facing outward caught her attention. The drawing on the cover was mysterious. There was a moon and water and a man gazing out to sea at a green light. *The Great Gatsby.* She held it up and the saleswoman nodded that she could take it.

As the next important item of business, she needed another spot to spend her solitary day.

"The bench by the river is perfect," she grumbled, "room for only one and far away from where someone might stop to admire the view." And what a view it was. Fortuna had grown to love the river as a living thing. Its eternalness comforted her. She thrilled to its torrents after a good rain and worried for its health in the dry months. She would miss it.

She passed a very narrow residential street with hardly room for two cars to pass. She looked at the street sign and laughed: "Hollywood Street. Sounds like there is a story there. But I will be too visible walking past all those kitchen windows just a few feet away."

She knew she presented a strange picture in this neighborhood. A bit further on, there was a narrow vacant lot stretching nearly a half mile all the way to Rio Grande Blvd. with a single overgrown tree hanging over the crumbling adobe wall on the south side. The sun was blazing now and Fortuna instinctively headed for the only shade in sight.

The day passed slowly under the tree, as Fortuna struggled to adapt her plan to the new reality.

"Just as I found a good place, somebody gets killed. You know I can't go back to the shelter, Abuela, especially now. I have to dodge the cops and Diego and his friends. This feels like a big setback."

When she arrived in Albuquerque in a van from the casino up north, she had the old rolling suitcase filled with her favorite books, a few clothes and toiletries and a gun. She had forty-three dollars and a broken arm that had not healed properly. She found her way to St. Bridget's but knew she could not stay in shelters for very long. As soon as her first money order arrived at her son Armando's house, Diego would know she was in Albuquerque and would be looking for her. If he had discovered she had taken a pistol from his gun closet, there would be more than a broken arm to pay.

"What happened to Diego? He wasn't mean when we married. He came back from Viet Nam in one piece, unlike Luisito and Herman. They were inseparable before shipping out, but only Diego and Luisito came back and Luisito will never get out of that wheelchair. Diego was the lucky one."

But a run of bad luck twenty years later—a failed harvest, which forced him to find a job, and a dislocated shoulder that caused him daily pain—had turned him vindictive instead of just indifferent as before. The young social worker at the hospital seemed to have her own problems so she took Fortuna's word that her broken arm was an accident and helped her apply for disability, allowing her to plan her escape.

"Diego doesn't know Albuquerque," she told Ofelia. "He would only look in the most obvious places. Not many days off working maintenance at the casino. Besides, he can't stay away too long from the hometown bars where his credit is good."

Fortuna spent her first months in Albuquerque at various homeless shelters, but was always searching for other places to spend the nights when it got warmer.Soup kitchens were a necessity until her disability checks started arriving at her Albuquerque post office box. She spent her days in the parks or in the coolness of the Old Town Plaza, where old trees shaded the wrought iron benches. Then one day in April she walked down Central to the river and discovered her bench. It had been her refuge, every day and also on many nights. But now with the police in the picture, the bench, the Plaza and the parks would all be too dangerous, too obvious. She needed to be less conspicuous.

"Since nobody comes here, no one should notice me here but after dark it might be dangerous. I saw a stray dog a while ago, but this field of dirt wouldn't appeal to strollers."

No sooner had she made this observation, a man came after his dog who would not come back to the road. The man did not look at her directly. Sitting on her suitcase, she supposed she looked like a typical homeless person and New Mexicans looked away from such hardships while praying to escape it.

Fortuna herself tried not to dwell on her own precarious position. She had very little income and most of what she had she sent up north for her grandson Billy, who deserved another chance to build a life when he got out of the county jail, where he was serving time for passing bad checks.

Fortuna knew that Ofelia would not approve of her plan. But she was his only hope.

"He has no one else to help him escape the life of so many young men up north," she said. My son Armando was a poor example. Mama always said boys should be given their head so I didn't speak up about his behavior until it was way too late. I had already lost him."

Armando dropped out of high school and spent his days drinking in a friend's trailer and began accumulating DWIs. He was too proud to go to rehab and had lost his driver's license before he turned twenty-one. He got temporary jobs from time to time, but tended to neglect bills in favor of nights at the bar. The only thing he did right was to marry the loyal and long-suffering Olivia, who was Fortuna's only ally in helping Billy escape a similar life.

Thinking about helping Billy gave her a boost of energy and she hugged the tree trunk to stand, stretched her sore back and headed east.

Could she take a chance on one last meal at the Good Shepherd soup kitchen? Until the police arrested the young man from the river, she would have to stay out of sight. How long could that take?

A few hours later, she headed back to the park, hoping to find her spot from the night before. But cutting through the park from the museums, she could see she was out of luck. A couple was camped underneath the tree and had spread a blanket to sleep on.

"Those fools will be evicted later on, but it will be too late for me to reclaim the spot," she said.

She crossed back through the park and entered the narrow streets of Old Town. She reached the corner of the block where Indian jewelry vendors were gathering their wares and blankets, wrapping up their day of haggling with tourists when a long black car pulled slowly alongside her.

"Black tinted windows too," she told Ofelia. "It looks like the cars of some of Armando's lowrider friends, except plain. The cars up north have saints and flames."

Even with the windows closed, a pounding bassline could be felt blocks away. And everyone within a block radius could hear the words of the hypnotic refrain:

"Gonna take my horse to the old town road/Gonna ride till I can't no more."

A young woman jumped out of the back seat and took several pictures of herself on the empty corner. She had long, straight black hair, dark skin and looked Indian. After a lifetime of being uncommonly dark, Fortuna always noticed shades of skin. She was called "negrita" as a child. Some said it affectionately. Just teasing, they said when she cried. But she knew in her heart that it was something significant and that it brought no gifts.

"What is she doing, abuela? Why did she take a photo there?"

She squinted at the green street sign on a pole: Old Town Road. Ever since she was a young woman, Fortuna paid close attention to coincidences. She believed them to signify something, but she could seldom figure exactly what that was. The car drove off. She would have to stop and rest in a safe place and think about it further.

Fortuna crossed the street and pulled open the heavy wooden door of the old Catholic church. She was relieved to see it was empty so she could think and talk to Ofelia. When in company, she feared that other people in the room could hear her thoughts.

"Abuela, think of all the people through the centuries who brought their troubles here."

Fortuna did not pray, she did not think God listened to her. She thought about her daughter, Esperanza, who fled the family for a new life in Mexico. Unlike Armando, she was dark-skinned like her mother and endured the same comments about it when she was young. One weekend,

Esperanza attended a health fair at the Sikh ashram in the Valley and never came home. Fortuna had visited her there once, but later received a letter saying she was going to Mexico to be married. Her guru, she said, had arranged it. She had not met her prospective husband. Fortuna tried to imagine her daughter's life in a faraway city.

"I hope she is happy with her husband but I wish I knew whether I have any grandchildren in Mexico. I have no way to contact her! I tried to get information at the ashram but they were not helpful. I guess families can be a problem."

Fortuna stayed in the coolness of the church until a caretaker came to lock up for the night, then sat in the courtyard of the old convent next door until sunset when she ventured back into the Plaza. A group of several dozen tourists had assembled under the portal of a restaurant across the street, listening to a tall, bearded man serving as their ghost tour guide. The Old Town Plaza was continuously inhabited for more than three hundred years and tales of ghost sightings went back almost as long. Attempting to scare tourists with the doings of the supernatural beings inhabiting some of the oldest of the adobe houses in the neighborhood was a nightly ritual.

Fortuna kept walking. Life held so many things more frightening than ghosts.

"I can't stay on the Plaza, abuela. The cops keep watch over the tourist dollars. I can't go back to the vacant lot. It was deserted even in the daytime, and now it's too dark and probably dangerous."

She could barely make out the branches of the lone tree, swaying in the nighttime breeze. There were benches along some of the side streets in Old Town, but they were all well-lit and No Loitering signs were posted here and there. Heading north would take her to the highway overpass, a popular spot for other homeless souls. But there had been robberies and assaults there too. To the south was Central Avenue, a dangerous place for anyone at night.

"Help me, Ofelia, where should I go?"

She stood on the sidewalk, willing her brain to come up with a plan. Suddenly, across the street, the answer appeared: a small, wrought-iron bench under a honey locust tree that nearly obscured it from her view. A tall trash bin hid it from another angle. But its best feature was that it did not face the street, unlike every other bench in Old Town. This one faced the parking lot of a rambling complex of adobe houses without yards, so there were few cars and no children. On this bench, just beyond the reach of a streetlight, she might even be able to sleep a bit. Old Town was deserted by tourists after the shops closed and passing cars would not notice her sitting there. As she hurried to cross the street between cars, she thanked her beloved Ofelia and the universe. It was perfect.

When Gus finally heard the car pulling away from his front door in the morning, he sat down hard on the couch and dropped his head into his hands. He had to tolerate some bad houseguests in the past, but this couple was the very worst. His uncle in Santa Fe, who owned the ramshackle adobe, let him live there for the price of utilities, but this was the downside of the deal. Whenever Tio Manuel needed to do someone a favor, which was increasingly often, Gus had to play host to assorted characters, some of them irritating and all of them in his way. Gus was on a mission to rebuild his life.

He started sweeping potato chip crumbs from the couch into his hand, but most of them went onto the rug, which was already strewn with fast food bags and empty Schlitz 40s. Gus had warned them not to bring alcohol into the house. So much for house rules. The pair had appeared two nights ago. They took over both the spare bedroom and the living room and drank and quarreled and watched loud reality TV with only rare breaks to walk down to LotaBurger or drive to the grocery store up on 12th Street.

Gus loved his uncle, who had always watched out for him. When he needed a fresh start away from the influences of his homies in Santa Fe, his uncle had fortuitously just evicted his previous tenants from the house.

"They couldn't even be bothered to take the trash to the road," his uncle said." Garbage was being run over in the parking lot. They took no pride in where they lived. I will expect better from you, Gustavo."

The house was old, with a roof that leaked and badly in need of some plaster. Since it was set back from the street behind another building, Gus's uncle had written the house number in white paint over the front door. It looked like bad graffiti, so delivery people didn't always recognize it as an address.

The house was part of a warren of crumbling adobe casitas under a canopy of tall Chinese elms and locust trees. These dwellings were flanked by a row of shabby apartments to the north and a newer complex including a two-story building to the south, housing an art gallery on the ground floor and two apartments above. Most of the ground floor windows were covered with iron grillwork to deter break-ins. Some of the roofs to the north sported satellite dishes and the occasional swamp cooler.

The house where Gus now lived had been the family home of Tia Carmen, Tio Manuel's wife, who inherited it along with its hefty Old Town tax burden. She had died ten years ago, and Manuel had rented out the house ever since. It needed a lot of work but was in a desirable neighborhood. Manuel could be charging more rent to someone else, but then would not be able to use it as a hostel. Since it was a small house, he had a revolving door system, Gus had concluded. He suspected there was more to know about why his honest and hardworking uncle had so many social debts to repay, but Gus hadn't felt free to ask questions.

Behind the large front room was a small, grimy kitchen, tiny bath and two bedrooms. Gus had initially moved into the larger bedroom, but when the guests began to arrive with regularity, he decamped to the smaller one in back for a little privacy. There was no question of quiet, the interlopers rarely cared that Gus had to be at work at eight.

He grabbed his keys and looked around. Cleaning up the mess would have to wait until he finished his shift cooking at the Central Avenue Diner. His boss had seemed pleased with him lately and he didn't want to mess that up. His counselor at rehab had encouraged him to think bigger about his life

"Maybe I could be promoted to kitchen supervisor," he told his uncle. "If I could make a little more money, I can move into my own apartment." And avoid having a parade of increasingly infuriating short-term roommates, he added silently. Maybe when he had won her trust, his dream girl Julia might visit him there. Maybe he could even afford a car, he thought as he walked down Central Avenue. Or a bicycle anyway.

When he got to work, the breakfast rush was in full swing. A new waitress, Lorena, smiled at him as she carried a tray of coffee cups to a table by the front window. He knew she was sweet on him, but his heart belonged to Julia. He nodded hello, went to the back, clocked in and grabbed a clean apron from his locker. He wished he had gotten a few more hours sleep. But it was hard to relax with the bass from the old stereo system turned way up, shaking the walls of his room and thumping in his chest. He had emerged from his room to ask his so-called guests to turn it down and they agreed. But if they had lowered the volume, it was imperceptible.

Gus hoped he would be able to sleep tonight. His uncle usually gave him a little notice before springing new arrivals on him. They had spoken the day before about the last one, who was apparently a friend of one of Gus's cousins. He had never been close to those cousins, although they had all gone down the same path of alcohol and drug abuse. But he had never heard of any of them going to rehab. Gus had gone three times. Hopefully the last one would stick.

"Alcohol, it's our family problem," his uncle said. "I know you youngsters take drugs too, but even us viejitos either had to eventually get sober or die in a car accident or when our bodies just gave out."

Gus had grown up in a middle class neighborhood in Santa Fe, in a house his mother bought with her insurance settlement after his dad died in a fiery wreck on I-25. His mother was a trained beautician, but could only work from home because she couldn't afford child care for Gus and his three sisters. They didn't go hungry, but there was little money left over for clothes and toys. They grew up feeling deprived, compared to the other children on the block. So when they were old enough to commit petty thefts, they felt entitled to do it. Gus put his friend Tommy's red Hot Wheels car in his pocket one day, but was afraid to play with it when anyone else was around. No one in his house would have cared that he stole it, but they might have tried to sell it.

When Gus was nine, his mother accompanied her boyfriend to a drug deal behind an empty storefront and was killed with a gunshot to the head. By then, her pretty face had been transformed by years of drug and alcohol abuse. Gus had loved her fiercely and mourned her deeply. He and his sisters were split up and went to live with various relatives.

Gus went initially to an aunt and uncle who lived in a mountain village up north, but he was angry and did not adjust well to such a lonely life. After a few months, another aunt in the bigger town down in the valley took him in. This time, there were older cousins to buffer his loneliness and minimal supervision by their working mother. Out of gratitude to his new-found companions, he soon joined in their activities.

"Orale Gus, see that guy who just got out of his truck? The one heading to the package store. See if he will buy us Forties! We can drink them in the woods along the river." As time went on, they graduated to marijuana and eventually, to heroin, both plentiful and cheap in the Valley. Gus got his driver's license at sixteen, and lost it before he turned eighteen after a string of DWIs he got while driving his aunt's car. The last time he was stopped, there were also drugs in the car.

As part of his plea bargain, he went to rehab. He spent thirty days at Delancey Street in Alcalde and intended to stay clean when he got out, but back in his old surroundings he soon relapsed. He did a stint in another rehab the following year with similar results. That's when Tio Manuel stepped in.

Back in Santa Fe without a car, Gus disconnected with his running buddies up north. His uncle rented him a room in his house, got him a construction job and drove him to AA meetings. He seemed to be adjusting to the straight life. But a year later he was furloughed from his job and with time on his hands, found a bar within walking distance of the house.

Events unwound as could be expected, and Gus found himself back in rehab. But that was where he met Julia. Serious and shy, she was not like the other girls in rehab; she didn't have the tough shell.

Julia had become dependent on OxyContin after breaking a leg in a car accident and that had led to heroin. From his first glimpse of her, Gus was entranced. She was a beautiful girl and he found himself stealing glances at her during group therapy. To his surprise and delight, she seemed drawn to him, after he spoke about how his uncle had saved him from himself years ago and his sadness at having disappointed him. He and Julia became friends, but she was discharged a few weeks later.

"When I get out, I want to see you…get to know you better," he said.

Julia looked uncomfortable.

"I will go out with you only if you stay clean for a year."

Here was the reason he needed to walk the straight line and he happily agreed. A year would give him time to build a life for himself, get a job. With his uncle's help, he moved away from bad company again, this time to Albuquerque.

Later in the day, Gus was in the back helping to put together a complicated lunch order for a large group when he heard what sounded like two gunshots. Hurrying out of the kitchen, he watched half of the people in the diner get up and rush to the front windows.

"Que paso? Que paso?" said an old man at the counter, who could not see past the people standing in front of him.

"He just shot that guy!" cried a woman who had just come in the front door. "He grabbed the bike and shot him!"

Gus pushed through the crowd to where he could see the street. A man lay on the ground with blood on his shirtfront. People on the street were pointing down Central towards the river. On the other side of the street, Gus could see a figure in black on a silver bicycle, heading west.

"Call nine-one-one!" someone yelled. But one of the bystanders on the sidewalk must have called already because the first police car arrived minutes later, lights flashing, followed by an ambulance and several other police cars. Two of the cars sped up Central towards where the gunman had disappeared on the bike.

One of the first officers on the scene stood at the door of the diner to prevent anyone else from coming outside, while another one squatted down by the victim, feeling for a pulse. Gus was pretty sure he was dead; there was a lot of blood and his eyes were open and fixed. When the paramedics arrived, they confirmed that he was deceased.

By this time, the scene inside the diner had become chaotic. People were shouting, demanding to be let out the door and several women were crying. A tall cop entered and pushed back the crowd. He had to shout to be heard over the commotion.

"We will need to talk to each of you," he said. "Whether or not you saw what happened, you may have other important information. We will have to ask you to stay until we can talk to you."

A waitress came out from behind the counter and tried to comfort one sobbing woman, sitting her down at an open booth and bringing her a glass of water.

"There were shots and... and...and he was covered with blood!" the woman said, gasping and wiping her nose with the sleeve of her shirt. The decibel level fell a bit as the shell-shocked patrons returned to their tables to await their turn to speak to the police. Most of them passed the time on their phones, rehearsing their statements on Twitter and Facebook.

The diner closed for business, but Gus had to stay until the police had finished with all the possible witnesses several hours later. He considered texting Julia, but they had agreed not to do that too often, so he refrained. Julia said he needed to be happy by himself before he could be happy with another person, so he tried not to appear too needy, even when he felt needy.

Instead of going home, Gus headed down Central towards where the shooter had disappeared on his victim's bicycle. When he reached the parking lot for the BioPark, he could see the lights of the police cars ahead at the roadblock. They had pushed the bystanders back to the strip mall but a few dozen die-hards were lingering and sharing the general opinion that the suspect had eluded police, crossed the river and was hiding in the Bosque.

"They'll get him," one old man said. "Where can he go? Even if he drowned in the river, they'll find him."

Gus was tired and his feet hurt from walking. He headed back to the house, cutting through back alleys behind the strip mall.

When he got home, he turned on the news and learned that the police had still not found the killer, who reportedly had shot the victim because he would not give up his bike. According to the on-scene reporter, the killer rode the bike to the river, then jumped in. The news footage showed helicopters circling the area where he disappeared and boats patrolling the river banks. But the killer, described only as young, of medium height and wearing black jeans and a black t-shirt, had seemingly vanished into the thickets of the Bosque.

Gus flipped through the television channels but couldn't find any more local news. He went into the kitchen and found a few slices of pizza in the refrigerator. They were not too old, leftovers from the unwanted visitors the night before. Gus nuked them for a minute in the microwave, then brought them back to the living room. He turned on the PS 3 and played Resident Evil for a couple of hours.

He really liked living in his uncle's house, he just wished the visitors weren't so sketchy. Most of them he didn't trust and he hid his PlayStation in a drawer in his room when he had to leave them in the house. He preferred being in the front of the house, closer to the front door and the street. It felt less safe in the back since there was no back door. As was his habit when he had the place to himself, Gus fell asleep on the couch and slept through the night.

The next morning he overslept. He took a quick shower and jogged the two blocks to the diner, arriving out of breath. The place was packed and humming with speculation and gossip about the drama of the day before. There were still traces of blood on the sidewalk out front.

"They still have the bridge blocked off," said Lorenzo the cook, who lived west of the river. "I had to cross over on Bridge Street, traffic was all fucked up. I guess they didn't find the guy yet. APD no vale nada."

"I went down there yesterday," Gus said. "They had boats and helicopters, it was like an army down there. I can't believe they couldn't find one guy on foot."

In the course of his shift, Gus heard any number of theories about where they killer went and why the cops couldn't find him. The bosque was a wild place with many places to hide.

"There are camps of homeless in there," said Lorenzo, flipping burgers on his industrial-size stovetop. "They build little shelters that they can take down easily when the cops come to get them out. Probably because some hiker complained. And sometimes kids set fires in the bosque. That clears them out."

Hours later, Gus was getting ready to clock out when his cell phone buzzed in his pocket. He hoped it was Julia. He had texted her last night about the murder but she hadn't responded. He looked at his phone and sighed. It was from his uncle.

"Very important," it read. "At nine tonight turn off outside lights and unlock the door. Call me when he's there."

"Who is coming?" he texted back. This was an unwelcome development. He was looking forward to having the place to himself for another night. Now this mystery guest. Shit.

"Just call me when he's there. We'll talk."

Tio Manuel had never given him so little information nor so little notice about a houseguest and he had a bad feeling about it. Shortly before nine, he looked through the iron bars on the front windows but the parking lot was still. Judging from the number of cars, everyone across the way was home for the night. There was a row of lights outside those units that burned all night. Gus stepped outside and saw a figure sitting on the bench by the road. A viejita, he thought. Why was she there? Did she have something to do with the mysterious visitor? He started to walk towards the bench, but when a car passed and spilled light onto her for a few seconds, he could see she seemed to be asleep, sitting up. He retreated back to the house and turned out the lights. The space before his front door went black. There was no moon tonight. Gus sat on the couch and turned off all the inside lights and also the television so he could hear someone approaching. He could hear his heart beating. A dog barked a few houses away but otherwise the neighborhood was quiet.

It was close to ten when he heard footsteps, someone running and breathing hard. The door flew open and a shadowy figure stood outside, panting and shaking. Gus jumped up and pulled the boy into the house, slamming the door shut.

Leo

eo woke up with a pounding headache and what felt like a mouthful of old socks. Opening his eyes a crack, he guessed he was in someone's living room, lying on the floor. At least he had kept his clothes on this time. He probably shouldn't have gotten into Tino's car in Santa Fe last night, but he heard something about a party at UNM. When the party proved too tame for Leo—lots of beer and pot but nothing more serious—he had made his way to Central Avenue, where he assumed he could find whatever he needed.

Buyers and sellers had ways of recognizing each other without referrals or introductions. So he quickly found a UNM student who knew a guy in the South Valley and they scored enough to knock at least one of them out, apparently. But now he was alone in a strange house and couldn't seem to locate his phone.

He told himself he should have stayed in Santa Fe, where he knew dealers and also older guys who would give him money in exchange for a blow job. Leo was not gay and he hated doing it, but he couldn't seem to hang onto any of the jobs his father had arranged since he graduated from high school ten years ago. The problem was that Leo didn't have any career interests except to make money but he didn't know exactly how to go about it. So while he was figuring that out, he tried to stay medicated. His saving grace was that he had such a fear of prison that he would not get involved in selling drugs. But he spent all of the money he could earn or steal buying them.

He cracked open the blinds an inch and could see he wouldn't be leaving through the front door. Too much traffic for his headache. It was really hot too, as he discovered when he exited through the backyard. How did people stand this, he wondered. Santa Fe was ten degrees cooler at all times. There were less students on campus during the summer months, but Leo had a vague recollection that the kid at whose house he had crashed said he was in summer school. He needed to find that kid. He also needed a ride back to Santa Fe but mostly, he needed a fix. And to find his phone.

He walked two blocks to the entrance of the main campus, trying to guess which buildings might have classrooms. He wasn't quite sure what his plan was, but without his phone his options were limited. Like most people his age, he didn't know how to find a phone number and use a landline. He didn't remember ever seeing anyone do that, except his mother, long before they moved to New Mexico.

Leo found that when it came to his mother, he remembered less and less every year. She had been a New York socialite married to a Wall Street mogul when Leo was born. He did remember that when he was a little boy, she would always say "Like Leonardo di Caprio, not Da Vinci" when introducing him to anyone.

His mother had a restless temperament and when Leo was a preteen, she convinced his father to move to Santa Fe, where she expected to find a more interesting life. Together, they found an old building near Canyon Road and opened the Tucker Sloan art gallery, which attracted a lot of interest from the start. His mother knew how to throw a party and every gallery opening had great food, an open bar, and a few celebrity guests.

Leo started working the openings during high school.

'You need to earn your spending money, learn the value of a dollar," his father said. Despite this proclamation, he was paid lavishly for being a go-for, so he learned to like and expect easy money. The no-sweat job offered his first easy access to alcohol. There was never any booze in the house since his father was a recovering alcoholic who attended AA meetings regularly. Somehow he failed to anticipate how easy it would be for his son to follow in his footsteps.

At first, Leo would consume the dregs in wine glasses he was bussing to the kitchen, but soon he had figured out how to take a tray of filled glasses and on his way back out to the reception, stash a couple in a hall closet. He would consume those whenever he found the hall deserted. He discovered to his delight and surprise that he could hold his liquor, never puking or passing out or otherwise betraying his burgeoning addiction. Then one night as a reception for a young Native American sculptor was winding down, Leo took some trash bags to the dumpsters behind the gallery and came upon his mother wrapped in the arms of the young artist.

The lovers did not see him and he took the bags back inside the gallery. Within a month, his mother was gone, back to New York City where she hoped her social contacts would advance her new boyfriend's career.

Leo tried not so show how hurt he was and how much he missed his mom. But he acted out his distress in a variety of unhealthy ways. At his expensive prep school, he hung with the rich druggies who always had enough coke to stand him a line now and then when funds were low.

One night during Christmas vacation, his homie proposed an adventure.

"There are so many of these adobe mansions around. I know a few where the family is skiing in Aspen or Vail or somewhere. It will be cool to break in and just look around. If we steal something we'll probably get caught eventually, but maybe we should just eat something and leave the evidence so they'll be freaked out when they get back."

They were excited to be doing something so bold and lawless. The adventure turned tragic when the owners' housekeeper woke up to strange people in the house and promptly had a massive heart attack and died before the paramedics arrived. They all went to court and their rich parents tried to work out plea deals with the DA so they could be sentenced to community service, but the judge sent them all to the New Mexico Boys School in the wilds of the Cimarron mountains. At the Boys' School for two years, Leo learned useful criminal skills and developed an immunity to shame or compassion.

The story had made the local papers so when he got out, Leo found that his criminal past was a major obstacle to finding jobs, even though his juvenile record was sealed. This made him once more dependent on his father to employ him, an arrangement they both resented. His wages were not generous, so he couldn't afford to buy his own cocaine. To get back at his parents and at his own off-the-tracks life, he decided to try heroin, which was cheap and offered oblivion, hopefully just short of death. Now, years later, it was the organizing principle of his life: finding it, using it, then finding the money to do it again. Which brought him to his present predicament.

The sun was beating down on him as he crossed the broad lawn towards the main summer classroom building. He was sweating and feeling dizzy as he climbed the stairs. When he pulled open the heavy door, cold air rushed out and smacked him in the face. The dizziness passed. He walked down the hall, peering into each classroom looking for a familiar face. He found one at the end of the hall.

It was a large hall with only a couple dozen students listening to an astronomy lecture. Luckily, the kid he was looking for was sitting near the back. Leo entered as unobtrusively as possible, sitting down behind the kid, whose name he couldn't remember.

"Hey man," he whispered, "I lost my phone and need to find my ride back to Santa Fe."

The kid motioned for him to go out into the hallway.

"Dude, you gave your phone to that girl who wanted to look at your pictures," he said. "Your phone is probably at Ramon's trailer, where we scored last night."

"I need to get back there and find my phone," Leo said. "I also have no money. Can you give me a ride?"

"No, dude, I can't. Not until my class is over," the kid said. "If you're in a hurry I'll give you directions and money for the bus.

The bus? Leo couldn't remember the last time he rode a bus. He had no idea how to do it.

The kid, whose house he had crashed at and whose name he still did not know, told him where to catch the Central Avenue bus heading west that would turn south on Atrisco and take him to the South Valley and Ramon's trailer. He handed him a five dollar bill.

"I need to get back to class," he said.

Leo had been hoping for more than a five dollar loan. What if he had to take a bus back to Santa Fe? He headed back to the kid's apartment. Maybe he would find something there he could sell. The back door was still open. Passing through the kitchen, he grabbed a strawberry Pop Tart from a box on the counter, tore open the wrapper and choked it down cold. He was not hungry, but who knew when there would be time to eat. One thing he had learned from his buddies in Santa Fe, you couldn't stay on the drug train without forcing yourself to eat.

"Gotta eat to keep your head," his friend Ziggy would say.

Leo started going through drawers in the biggest bedroom, looking for cash. No luck. He went into one of the smaller rooms and looked through more drawers and backpacks. He was getting discouraged when he found a fifty dollar bill inside a birthday card. That would get him home. There was a shoebox on a shelf in the closet of another bedroom and he secretly hoped for another cash bonanza, but it was even better: it held a small handgun. He could definitely sell that. But first he needed to get to Ramon's, retrieve his phone and find a fix. Then he would worry about getting back to Santa Fe. He shoved the gun into his pocket, put the box back on the shelf and closed the closet door. He needed to get to the goddam bus.

Leo was too sick and dizzy to run, but he walked back to Central Avenue as fast as he could. At the bus stop, he sat down on a bench in the shade for a minute, but he was too buggy to sit still. He paced the sidewalk until the dizziness took over and he sat down again. Two old women with rolling shopping carts had arrived at the bus stop and were sitting on the bench. They looked at him warily and scooted away.

I guess I look like shit, Leo thought. Can hardly blame them. Lucky for him, he had a round, youthful face and a slight build so even with the after effects of the night before, he didn't look particularly dangerous. If they only knew, he thought, feeling the gun in his pocket. It really is cold steel, he thought. Guns were one thing he had been able to avoid so far. The drug dealers he bought from were other prep school kids and guns weren't part of the conversation.

Leo's head ached and he couldn't remember the number of the bus he was supposed to take, but the one that came said Central Avenue and that's where he needed to go so he boarded, gave the driver the five dollars, jammed the change in his pocket and went to the very back of the bus, even though there were less than a half dozen other passengers. Now he was sweating and shaking and didn't want to be watched. The bus's progress slowed considerably when they reached downtown. There was a lot of slow-moving traffic and Leo was becoming anxious. The dope sickness was coming on hard. Ramon had better be home, he thought. He would need something before he could return to Santa Fe. Everything would have been so much easier if he had his phone.

Finally they left downtown and headed for Old Town, a mile or two further west. As the bus approached the stoplights at Rio Grande Blvd., the driver put on his right turn signal. Leo jumped up. He couldn't go north, he needed to stay on Central, cross the river and turn south on Atrisco. He had boarded the wrong bus after all. When the driver stopped to pick up a passenger at the corner, Leo stumbled off, clutching his stomach, which was beginning to spasm. He looked down Central for another bus, but there were none in sight. He would never make it to Ramon's on foot. Then he saw the solution to his problem. Across the street, a middle-aged man stood at the eastbound bus stop in front of a diner with his hand on a silver bicycle. Leo staggered across the street and wordlessly grabbed the bike. But the man was stronger than Leo had calculated, plus he was not suffering from drug sickness. He pulled back.

"What are you doing?" he yelped.

Leo saw red, literally. He needed that bike. It was his last chance. His hand went into his pocket and pulled out the gun. He aimed it at the leg of the man with the bike and pulled the trigger. It was easy. As the man stumbled backward and fell, he let go of the bike. Leo jammed the gun into his pants, got on the bike and started pedaling as hard as he could towards the river. A woman screamed and some people yelled and chased him, but they were on foot and then he was across the street and into the bike lane. He felt weak, but realized this was his only chance at escaping and finding a fix. He hoped he hadn't seriously hurt the guy but couldn't turn to see if he had gotten up. He knew the cops would be coming soon and they would have cars, so he needed to get off the street. When he approached the bridge, he could see a bike path through the trees and he took it down to the river. The river was running low. People drowned in the Rio all the time when it was running high and fast but there was a drought in New Mexico and so far the runoff from the mountains had been weak. He stopped at the riverbank with his eyes on the tangle of trees and bushes on the other side. He knew there were hiding places in there where he could lay low until dark. He couldn't risk trying to get to Ramon's trailer now, it was too far.

He dropped the bike on the bank and started to run across the muddy streams running beside islands of sand revealed by the low water. As he approached the first island, he slipped on the muddy river bottom and fell. The river swept him along for a few yards before he regained his footing and made it the rest of the way across. He only looked back once before entering the trees. He saw a woman sitting on a bench on the bridge with a large rainbow umbrella. She seemed to be looking right at him.

When he got past the first line of trees, Leo started looking for a place to hide. There were fallen trees and hollow logs everywhere and lots of underbrush to cover himself with. They would be coming for him and he was too sick to run any farther. He stumbled past a wide thicket of chamisa, their pungent smell made him sick and he threw up the Pop Tart. He could not get arrested and go cold turkey in jail. He climbed over a downed cottonwood and spotted a series of hollow logs piled up together so it was hard to see inside them. The one on the bottom, partially obscured by bushes and other vegetation, looked big enough for him to fit inside. He couldn't see the other side of the river anymore, but he could hear the sirens. He tried not to think about snakes. The bosque was probably crawling with them but he had no other choice. He wriggled inside the log, feet first, and scraped all the leaves he could reach over the entrance. He hoped the shaking and dry heaves would not give him away. He hoped the cops were afraid of snakes too.

The hours that followed were the longest he had ever spent. Leo had been in some jams before, but hell was where he was now. There was noise from the river and the air and he was aware of groups of searchers passing by, but they did not find him. Eventually, night began to fall. The heat pulled back a bit and the crickets quieted down. When it was full dark, Leo wriggled out of his log. He saw that his arms were covered in bug bites but he couldn't feel the itch, his misery was so much greater. He limped to the edge of the trees and saw no patrols.

He could tell by the lights that the bridge was still blockaded and all the cops were congregated there. Why were they making such a big deal out of a stolen bicycle? He went back to the hollow log, took the gun from his pocket and shoved it as far into the opening as he could reach. He might need it again but it was too dangerous to have now. He moved slowly across an unlit dirt parking lot, trying not to stagger or fall and draw attention to himself. Beyond the lot was a strip mall with untended land behind. Once he got to those weeds, he was invisible. He stayed in the weeds until he reached Atrisco where he cut down to the trailer park.

Leo walked down the line of single-wides, trying to remember what Ramon's looked like. In the dark, all of them looked the same. He didn't know what cars might be parked there. He was about to start shouting Ramon's name when he noticed a red tricycle with a flat tire next to some trash bins. That looked familiar. Leo didn't pray but he asked the universe to please please let Ramon be home and let him still have Leo's phone.

He knocked on the door, waited a few seconds and when he didn't hear anyone coming to open the door, started to bang on it with both fists.

"Ramon! Come on man you got my phone," Leo pleaded. He had

to score to be able to get himself back to Santa Fe, so he thought better of breaking in. That would not improve his standing with Ramon. He sat down on the box that served as a step to enter the trailer. His brain wasn't functioning at all anymore, he had no other plan.

After a few minutes, he heard footsteps inside the trailer. Ramon opened the door, he was in his underwear and didn't look happy.

"Chinga tu madre," he said. "and chinga your phone. I'm busy."

"Ramoncito, where did you go?" A girl's voice called from the bedroom.

Leo stepped into the door and scanned the room for the phone. There were clothes and food containers strewn everywhere. Ramon moved some damp towels from one end of the couch and the phone was there, tucked between the cushions.

"Take your phone and fuck off," said Ramon.

Leo pulled the fifty dollars from his pocket and held it out to Ramon.

"Please, I'm sick," he said. "I'll give you fifty dollars for just a taste so I can get home."

Ramon grabbed the bill from his outstretched hand and walked back into the bedroom. Leo heard a drawer slam and Ramon came back with a bindle and threw it at Leo, who bent to grab it from the floor.

"Don't come back here," Ramon said, pushing Leo out of the trailer and slamming the door.

Leo sat down on the rickety stairs, unwrapped the bindle and snorted the contents. In seconds, he had stopped shaking, but he knew the effects would not last for long. Ramon, the stingy bastard, had taken his fifty dollars and given him a ten dollar hit. Now he would have to figure out another way to get back to Santa Fe. He would have to call his father and beg for his help. He wondered about the man whose bicycle he stole...the man he shot. How bad was he hurt? He was sure his father could fix it up. He had plenty of money and, like most rich people, political connections all over the state.

His father picked up on the second ring.

"Where are you dammit? I was worried." He was yelling.

"I'm in Albuquerque," Leo said. "I lost my phone so I couldn't call. I don't have any money and I'm in a bit of a jam."

"What kind of jam exactly?" His father had that here-we-go-again tone in his voice.

"I needed this bike and the guy didn't want to give it up and there was a gun. I might have shot him."

There was a silence on his father's end of the phone.

"Was that you?' He asked quietly. "Who killed a man in Old Town over a bicycle?"

"Oh shit," Leo said. "I didn't know he died. Oh shit. What should I do, Dad?" He had managed to avoid considering this possibility. Now he was looking at jail, not rehab.

"You could turn yourself in," his father said. "I'll get you a good lawyer. He might be able to get you a deal for lesser charges."

"I can't turn myself in, I'm sick. I'm dope sick. They'll make me go cold turkey in jail. There's got to be some other way. Just until I can get myself straight."

Another long silence. Then his father said, "I need to make some calls. Don't lose your phone again." And he hung up.

Leo walked south until he got to Bridge Street, then headed back towards the river. He crossed the bridge and climbed down into the vast, deserted railroad yards. There was a large building whose windows were all broken. The city was trying to interest a film company in taking it over but they hadn't closed the deal. Meanwhile, taggers and vandals had been at work and it was easy to get inside. Leo sat down on the concrete floor to wait for his father to call. Early the next morning, he finally did.

"There's a house on Rio Grande, just across from Old Town," his father said. "It's directly behind a wholesale jewelry store at three-fifty, same block as Sofia's restaurant. Go there tonight at nine. The lights will be off, make sure no one sees you there. The guy who lives there is Gus, he'll take care of you."

"Dad, will he have some drugs for me?" Leo sounded plaintive.

"Gus is related to Manuel, who works for me. You know him, he built the new studio," his father said. "The house belongs to Manuel but Gus lives there. Gus is clean. Don't be causing trouble there. He needs to stay clean to keep his job."

"But Dad, I'm going to need something."

"You're going to need to keep it together until I can figure something out."

Leo spent the day shaking on the dirty floor and as night fell, started walking towards Old Town, staying in the side streets and back alleys so no one would see him. That woman on the bridge, he thought, might have given a description. The cops might be looking for him right now. He kept his head down and avoided the well-lit streets until he crossed Central and headed towards the park. He crossed in the shadows, away from the streetlights. He avoided the Plaza but made his way to Rio Grande. He saw the sign for the jewelry store and the house behind it. There were well-lit houses to the south, but only a closed restaurant to the north so he jogged across the street and waited by the building that housed the store, eyeing the door to the house. There were no lights inside or out. He took a deep breath and ran across the narrow parking lot to the door and pounded on it until it flew open.

"Who are you? What the hell is going on?" Gus said. The boy looked like he was coming off some drug trip. Gus had seen enough of that in detox to be able to guess what was in store for him. This was even worse than he had feared.

"I need a place to stay," the boy said. "I'm sick."

"What's your name?" Gus asked.

"Leo," he said. "My father said to come here. Do you have chiba?"

"No way, man," Gus said. "You've come to the wrong place for that."

Leo sat down on the couch and put his head in his hands.

"I'm sick," he said. "I'm sick."

He looked sick, Gus thought.

"I need to call my uncle," he said.

Tio Manuel sounded relieved when he picked up.

"He's there?"

"Yes," Gus said. "But who is he and what am I supposed to do with him? He's looking for drugs and you know I can't be around that."

"Don't worry," his uncle said. "He won't be staying. He's going upstairs in Rumaldo's house, I'll tell you where to find the key."

Rumaldo was his uncle's friend who owned the house in front. On the street side, a sign hanging over the door indicated that it had once been a jewelry business but it was locked up now. Iron gates outside the windows and artificial plants inside obscured the interior and Gus hadn't seen anyone enter or leave in all the months he had been living in Albuquerque.

At the back of the building, a flight of stairs hidden behind a fence led to a blockhouse on the roof. Gus had never seen anyone climb up the stairs or enter the building at all, even when the burglar alarm went off, which happened from time to time. The alarm was very loud and tended to be set off at night when someone tried to break into the jewelry store. It took a long time for the alarm company to respond, and by then the Anglos upstairs across the parking lot would have called the police. The couple in the front had a baby and wouldn't put up with it for long. The disabled old lady in the back might be quick to call too if she didn't have hearing problems. Gus assumed that most old people did.

He remembered a conversation he overheard between his uncle and aunt when another of his uncle's tenants had left abruptly.

"They couldn't take it anymore. Benny cries and screams all night long," his uncle said. "He doesn't want to stay locked up but since Graciela died, there's no one to watch him. Rumaldo has his business to run."

He recalled hearing that Rumaldo had an autistic son. That must be Benny. But where did Benny go? He had never seen him

"What happened to Benny?" Gus asked. Tio Manuel was silent for a moment. He probably was unaware that Gus knew about Benny.

"Benny ran away a few years ago," Manuel said. "The family searched for him but he drowned in the Acequia Madre. Rumaldo closed the store soon after that.

"Listen to me, Gustavo. Under the stairs leading to the roof there are stones along the fence. The key to upstairs is under one of them. Take Leo up there and lock him in. There's a mattress up there and a toilet. The water had been turned off so you'll have to bring him a bucket of water so he can flush it. There's a bucket in the utility room. When you take him over, make sure there are no lights, and wait until late so there's no one around or awake."

"Tio, this guy needs a hospital or a detox, something," Gus said. "He's really sick."

"Well he's going to have to handle it himself," Manuel said. "He's my boss Tucker's kid, but he's in a lot of trouble. Better you don't know. Just get him out of the house and make sure nobody sees you."

"He's not going to want to stay up in that place," Gus said. "It sounds like a jail."

"Ya que," his uncle said. "He should have thought about that before. His father says we do this. He can take it up with him."

Gus hung up the call and turned to face Leo, who was lying on the couch with his hands over his eyes.

"You can't stay here," he said. "There a place upstairs across the way, I need to get the key and I'll take you up there."

Gus opened the door and looked around. The old lady on the bench hadn't moved. A breeze made the tree branches sway, but she didn't stir. Gus crossed the driveway and ducked under the stairs leading up to the room on the roof. He pried up the stones one by one until he found the key. It was caked with dirt and obviously hadn't been disturbed in a long time. He brushed off the dirt and put the key in his pocket. He went back in the house and went to the utility room, where the hot water heater stood next to piles of old telephone books topped by an old plastic bucket. He took it to the kitchen and started filling it up with water. He made a peanut butter sandwich and grabbed a bottle of water. Leo was still on the couch with his eyes closed. Gus couldn't let him fall asleep.

"Hey dude, wake up," he said. "Don't fall asleep there, it's not safe here. I'm taking you to the other house. C'mon and be quiet. The neighbors can't see you."

Leo sat up and followed him, eyes half shut. They crept across the twenty-foot driveway to the bottom of the staircase. Leo was swaying so Gus, carrying the bucket, went up the stairs behind him in case he started to fall. There were eighteen steps to the landing, where some flimsy railings were all that stood between them and the ground.

Gus put down the bucket. Leo tried to lean against one of the railings but it nearly gave way under his weight. Gus pushed him against the wall while he fumbled in his pocket for the key. When the door swung open, Gus stepped inside and flipped the light switch but the electricity had been cut off years before. Leo caught sight of the mattress lying in the corner and fell onto it without bothering to clear away the coat of dirt and dead roaches. Gus noticed that a window on the north side of the room had been left open an inch. All of the windows had bars. He put the bucket of water next to the commode standing by itself in a corner.

Gus put the sandwich and bottle of water on the floor by the mattress. "Here's some water and something to eat," he told Leo, but he couldn't tell if Leo heard him. " I'm going to lock you in so no one will bother you. The bucket of water will let you flush the toilet if you need to since there's no electric." Getting no response from Leo, Gus went out, locked the door and went down the stairs, trying to shake off a nagging feeling of being in over his head. It was hours before he fell into a restless sleep.

Rod

The light over the door of the house across the parking lot was never out, so when it turned off it caught Rod's attention. He had seen a fair number of sketchy people coming and going from the house along with one fairly normal-looking guy who seemed to live there fulltime. But in the six months he had worked at the gallery, Rod had never seen that light go off. There were so many lights on around the clock in this little complex, he had taken to wearing a sleep mask at night.

The bedroom was actually in the back of the space, behind the gallery, but that room had no windows at all and it felt claustrophobic. So he dragged a futon out to the front to sleep. Besides, sometimes customers came at night and he needed to hear them knock. Those were the best customers—easy to please and they always paid cash.

He was lying on the futon masturbating and fantasizing about a waitress at the casino where he used to work when the light went out. He finished quickly, then got up and stood by the French doors where he could watch through the blinds. No cars were parked in the driveway, which functioned as sort of a pass-through between the old houses and cheap row apartments to the north, and the newer structures on the south side.

There was an obvious class divide between the dwellings on his side of the pass-through and those on the other side: the people who lived upstairs and in the little houses to the west kept their yards tidied, had nice cars and drove them to work in the mornings. The tenants on the other side left disabled cars in their parking spaces, litter was strewn around their tiny yards and he rarely saw anyone leave for work. Welfare queens, he thought.

He opened the French doors and stepped out onto the breezeway. A hot wind was blowing and he turned to go back into the air conditioning inside the gallery, when he spotted a shadowy figure on the bench by the street. He took a few steps in that direction, trying to determine who it was but instead retreated inside. Rod made a point of not getting acquainted with his neighbors and tried to remain as anonymous as possible, given the nature of his business. He worried that they might notice the late night comings and goings and wonder what they signified, but so far they all seemed preoccupied with their own worries.

Upstairs on the street side was a young couple with a baby, in the back was an elderly woman who seemed to be disabled and rarely came downstairs. Rod once watched her painfully make her way to the mailbox using a cane and thought he should offer to check her mail for her occasionally, but thought better of it. The less contact he had with his neighbors, the better.

Rod was grateful for the job, which paid pretty well in addition to including free rent, so he tamped down his misgivings about what was behind it. People were paying a lot of money for mediocre paintings and all the customers were referred to his gallery by the owner, who Rod had only seen once. Clearly money was being laundered here.

The gallery was set back from the street so even though it was in Old Town, there was no foot traffic. There was no reason for any art lover to wander across the street to visit a gallery that was effectively hidden from the view of passersby.

Rod couldn't fathom how he had fallen so far so fast. He grew up in Denver in a middle class family. He was a celebrated jock in high school and took full advantage of the perks of his status. He dated two cheerleaders and sexually assaulted them both. But that was back in the days when girls who complained were shamed and shunned, so he never really paid a price for his crimes. There were rumors of course, the girls did talk to each other but by the time it began to seriously affect his social life, he graduated and moved on.

He attended the University of Denver and joined a fraternity where there were always drinks, drugs and coeds looking for love but willing to settle for sex. But those girls did expect to be taken home in the morning. They also expected to be called again. Rod found navigating the web of former and prospective not-really-girlfriends to be exhausting. So by the time he earned his MBA, he was spending his free time playing rugby and hanging with his buddies at Hooters.

After graduation, he went to work for the Denver Chamber of

Commerce with an idea of maybe going into politics. Starting out, he didn't want to work too hard but liked the idea of having a staff and being paid by taxpayers. Rod was then a very handsome young man; it took decades for his lifestyle to start showing on his face. But during his ten years rising to head up the Denver C of C, he rarely went home alone. Rod was especially successful with waitresses and strippers. He liked them stacked, but petite. Baby spinners, he called them.

"You just put them on top and spin them around," he said. Like most of the other men he knew, Rod was just amusing himself, but occasionally one of the spinners would get too attached and become a problem. One chick in particular showed up at his job. Rod presented himself at work as a serious professional and couldn't appear to be dating a Mexican Hooters waitress.

His solution was to take her to a coffee shop a few blocks away. He sat across from her in a booth. She gave him her prettiest smile, he did not return it.

'So what was it you wanted?"

"I just keep thinking about last night. It was so special," she said. "I have never felt like this. I think I'm falling in love with you."

Rod shook his head. He wasn't going to have this conversation.

"Baby, I have enjoyed fucking you, but let's get real here," he said. "You've been to two rodeos and a county fair, and so have I."

The girl sort of crumpled under his words. She sat there, stunned, for a minute, then fled to the ladies room. As soon as she disappeared, he slipped out the door and jogged back to his office. He needed to forget about the spinners, he thought. He needed to find a woman who could do more for him than take him to bed. Denver was filled with young professional women with good connections and making good money and most of them were also looking for love.

I can fake that, Rod figured, if it helped him get where he needed to go.

Six months later, he thought he had found the big score: a pretty lawyer with a trust fund who did some work for the Chamber. They moved from exchanging glances at meetings to lunch dates, where she hinted that there might be more. Things seemed to be going according to plan, until Rod got drunk at a Christmas party at the Chamber and backed her up against a wall, groping her clumsily. He missed the signs of resistance, and took it too far, reaching up her dress and under her thong underwear. Not only was the romance over, but the lawyer reported the incident to the police as an assault. His bosses fixed things up with the police department, but they also fired him and declined to give him a reference with which to find another job. Denver, where he hoped to ascend to political office one day, was finished for him.

Rod's Denver posse had no realistic suggestions for him.

"Maybe you could get a new identity, maybe move to Boulder where nobody knows you," suggested one friend. "You just need a plan, we'll all help."

But Rod liked being himself, even with a damaged reputation. Assuming another identity seemed like an awful lot of work, something he avoided whenever possible. He put his furniture in storage and prepared to leave town.

New Mexico seemed like a good place to get lost and start over. He had a buddy working on a movie set in Taos so he jumped in his red Fiat Spyder and headed south. He had no trouble getting hired on the film set, but the work was not glamorous. In fact, it was boring. He was a glorified security guard for a scene at the local rodeo grounds, wearing a red vest and shooing away curious bystanders. This went on for hours while the crew waited for the star to come out of his luxury bus in the parking lot. After a few weeks he was added to the roster of drivers and spent his days ferrying actors to and from the set. It was a higher-status job, but it was tourist season and traffic in the center of town was bumper-to-bumper pretty much all day long. Most of the cast stayed at La Fonda and there was no way to escape the gridlock.

After the movie wrapped, Rod hung around Taos for a few years, tending bar, living in a guesthouse on the estate of a rich elderly widow, and chatting up the nubile young women who hung out after hours on the Plaza. When he left work, he would join them, sharing their blunts and listening to their problems with parents and boyfriends. Now pushing forty, he feigned a fatherly vibe, but he knew they were tempting him and that eventually he would take one of them home.

"It must have been so fun working on the movies," cooed Carmelita, a big-eyed Hispana who always wore a crop top and Daisy Dukes and positioned herself so her breasts were on full display." I would love to hear more about it and maybe I can do that someday."

Rod caught the vibe and decided to stick around until the others left. He offered her a ride home. They made out in his car for a while, then went back to his place. There had not been much conversation so it was a surprise to him to discover a few days later that not only was she just seventeen, but she had three brothers. He tried to avoid her, heading straight home after work without visiting the Plaza. But hell hath no fury, and she understood she was being dumped and also ghosted. Now Taos was over for him too.

One afternoon at the bar a few months back, he spent an hour or two talking with a middle-aged woman from Pojoaque Pueblo, who was related to the Pueblo governor.

"I can get you a management job at the casino," she said. "They are always looking for smart, handsome men to bring in the women. I can talk to my cousin and fix it up." She made silver and turquoise jewelry and had left him her business card. He gave her a call, made an appointment to see her and headed south.

The woman did get him a job, but it was dealing blackjack for an hourly wage. Ten years later, the salaried position he had been led to expect had still not materialized. But as time went on, he came to appreciate the lack of responsibility that came with a job as a dealer. He had to watch his players, but whatever the other employees were doing was none of his affair. When his shift was over, he would cruise down the highway to a rival casino and head for the bar. It was the best place to spot candidates for that night's bed warmer. Luckily there were a lot of casinos in northern New Mexico, so he could always tap another if a particular woman became too much trouble.

Drifting off to sleep, he thought how he should have been satisfied with that life. If he had not been so eager to get rich quick he might not be sleeping on a mattress on the floor of an art gallery. And a fake art gallery at that.

F

Fortuna

Fortuna awoke from her slumber on the bench to see two shadows moving across the wide driveway between the two houses. A man and a boy, she thought, the man carrying something heavy in one hand. She didn't know if they could see her there in the shadows, but she pretended to be asleep just in case. They went out of sight while climbing the stairs, but then she saw a dark shape on the landing as Gus opened the door. After a few minutes, the shape appeared again at the top of the stairs. A minute later, Fortuna saw the man move across the driveway and enter the dark house. Maybe there was a commonplace explanation for what she had just seen, but the dark house and the furtiveness of the two did seem mysterious. And what exactly had awakened her?

Fortuna had always had an active imagination, and it was only fueled by the books she read as a young girl courtesy of the county bookmobile. In the mountain village where Fortuna grew up, there was no library and none of her neighbors had books on their shelves. But the first time the bookmobile stopped at the parking lot of the Senior Citizens Center, she begged her mother to let her go. Her mother saw little usefulness in any books but the Bible, but she was happy to have Fortuna out of her hair for a few hours.

After perusing the shelves inside the cramped van, she picked out *Black Beauty* for the picture of a rearing horse on the cover. She knew something about horses from living in the mountains and that one looked special. And black. For months after reading the book, she would pretend that she was Black Beauty and roamed the fields and paddocks where her neighbors kept their horses. In the story, Black Beauty was sold many times but after a cruel master, there was another who appreciated him and treated him kindly. When she returned *Black* Beauty, she found *Little Women*, with a picture of four frolicking girls on the cover But the lives of White girls who lived in New England a hundred and fifty years ago was something entirely new and unfamiliar. She liked the title, she would have liked to think of herself as a little woman instead of an ungainly girl. When she got into the atmosphere of the thing, she felt connected to the four sisters and their problems, and it was comforting to read about girls whose mother saw them clearly and cherished them all the same.

Fortuna craved her mother's approval, but rarely got it. She was one of six children and the only one who had inherited the dark skin of la Domenica, her father's great-great grandmother. Fortuna came to accept that since her appearance did not please her mother, she would be loved less than the others. Her sisters attended community college down in the Valley and got secretarial jobs, but there was never any discussion of a career for Fortuna. One night she heard them talking in the kitchen when she got up for a glass of water. They did not see her.

"The girls have good jobs and the boys have the chile and corn and the animals to fill their days. But what are we going to do with the negrita?" her mother asked. "She will graduate from high school this year."

Her father sighed. He loved his dark daughter but her future seemed uncertain. She had never had a boyfriend and spent all of her free time with her nose in a book. That would not help her find a husband. There was always work to be done, and books were a distraction. Besides, some of the notions she had picked up from books were better left unexamined.

She had recently gone through a Nancy Drew phase, reading all the volumes the bookmobile had about the teenage detective who always found mysteries to solve. Fortuna had become so observant of her neighbors in case there were curious circumstances that needed to be examined, that she earned a reputation for being nosy. She asked questions about everything and most of the inhabitants of her village found them intrusive and annoying. Marrying her off seemed a way to end her detective illusions by confronting her with some real world problems.

"Orlando's son is not too much older than Fortuna," he said. "He is very shy and is still single. Orlando worries that he will never give him the grandsons he wants. Maybe we can help them get acquainted without being too obvious."

With an unsubtle nudge from their families, Fortuna and Diego became acquainted and both seemed willing to settle for each other. Fortuna knew she would be hard pressed to escape the village without her family's support but she could escape her family by marrying Diego.

Besides, she could tell that her dusky mother-in-law approved of her much more than her own mother did. It was Ramona who taught her to cook. Her own mother had seemed to tire of schooling her daughters in domestic arts and by the time Fortuna was old enough to help, she preferred to cook alone.

For his part, Diego had never expected to marry. He didn't know what to say to girls and wasn't interested in learning. But if his family was going to deliver a wife with no effort required on his part, he would go along. She was very dark-skinned but tall and strong. It might be nice to have his own household and someone to do the chores.

So they were married and Fortuna had two babies in quick succession, Armando and Esperanza. There was no love between Fortuna and Diego, but at first he tolerated her escape into books as long as the house was clean and supper on the table when he came in from the fields. But as the years went on, it became an issue between them. People in the village gossiped about Fortuna's Bookmobile obsession and the men mocked Diego for allowing his wife such self-indulgence.

"If I caught my wife reading in the middle of the day, I'd throw the book away and find her some work to do," said his friend Emilio. "There are always walls to wash and weeds to pull. No good will come of all that reading."

But as the years went on and the children grew up, books were Fortuna's salvation, her escape and deliverance from the sameness of every day. A co-worker at the Head Start where Fortuna sometimes worked as a teacher's aide gave her special editions of *Jane Eyre* and *Wuthering Heights* illustrated with wood carvings of the most dramatic scenes. She loved those books and read them again and again, gazing at the pictures lost in dreams. She no longer dreamed of adventure for herself, but she hoped her children would be luckier and spun tales in her mind of their futures in some faraway land. It made her sad that neither Armando or Esperanza had inherited her passion for reading. Once television reception came to the village, the chance to interest them was gone.

"Ay Dios I can't think of those days," she said to Ofelia. "I need to tell myself a story—a good one—to push out those thoughts." But as she became drowsy on the bench it was that song she heard earlier on the Plaza that echoed in her brain.

"Gonna take my horse to the Old Town road/Gonna ride till I can't no more." There was something hypnotic about it and she allowed it to lull her to sleep.

A rhythmic pounding woke her. It stopped momentarily, then started again. The sun was coming up and the street and parking area were still deserted. She tried to guess the source of the noise and decided it was coming from the upper floor in the back of the house on the street. Trees obscured her view of the windows and the stairway and entrance, but she saw a half-dressed man emerge from the house across the driveway. He surveyed the area to see who else might have heard the pounding upstairs. He glanced at Fortuna on the bench, but she lowered her eyes, hoping it would signify her lack of curiosity. She was in no hurry to find another isolated place to spend her time so she took out *The Great Gatsby* and lost herself in that strange world.

Gus

Gus unlocked the door and Leo pulled it open. Being bigger than Leo and not strung out, Gus was able to push him back into the blockhouse and lock the door again but Leo began banging on the door again.

"Look man, if you stop making so much noise I'll see what I can do for you," Gus said. "But if you keep this up, the people across the parking lot will call the police. This shit doesn't happen in this neighborhood."

When the banging stopped, Gus went back to his house and called his boss to say he wouldn't be at work. In the months that he had been working at the diner, he had never taken a sick day. He took great pride in his perfect record. This kid was invading his life in any number of unacceptable ways. His job was the best thing he had going for him and there was no way he was getting involved in bringing this kid heroin. He had left that life behind forever.

He called his uncle.

"Oye tio, I have a real problem with this kid. He's banging on the door, says he's detoxing and sick. He's asking me to get him drugs and I can't do that. I don't know anybody who uses that shit and I can't take a chance on getting popped for something like that," he said. "It took me too long to get out of all that, I won't go back there."

"Okay hijo, I hear you," Manuel said. "Let me talk to Leo's father and see what he wants to do. I will leave you out of it."

"Tell him someone needs to watch him," Gus said. "I need to go to work. I called in sick today but I'm not doing that again."

"Okay Gustavo. I'll be in touch."

Gus sat down on the couch, hoping he would hear the phone ring before Leo started hammering on the door again. An hour later, his uncle called back.

"Tucker will take care of it," he said. "He's sending someone who will bring him some Oxycontin, that should settle him down until we can get him out of there. The guy should be there this afternoon and then you can go back to work. You need to start leaving the key outside again, where you found it. That way if someone comes with drugs for Leo, you don't have to be involved."

Gus was relieved, but worried about how he would handle a jonesing Leo for however long it took for the connection to get there. Leo was quiet at the moment, but that wouldn't last. After an hour, Gus went back up the stairs to the blockhouse. When he unlocked the door and looked in, Leo was sprawled out on the mattress shaking and sweating. Gus handed him the water bottle. Leo took a swallow, rinsed his mouth and spat the water on the floor.

"My dad says someone would bring some Oxy for me," he said. "Where is it?"

"Nobody has come yet," said Gus. "You're going to have to be patient."

Leo scowled.

"You must be kidding, man. I'm sick, my stomach is killing me and it's going to get worse."

"You don't have to tell me," said Gus. "I know all about it. I know about detox. That's why I don't touch the stuff anymore. When your dad's friend comes, I'll bring him up but you gotta stay up here for now.

"There's nothing you want in the house...no drugs and no alcohol so there's no point in going over there. Someone might see you. I know you went through the medicine cabinet in the bathroom last night. Didn't find anything, did you?"

Leo looked as if he wanted to hit him. He clenched and unclenched his fists, then turned and punched the wall. His knuckles started to bleed and he roared in pain.

"That was stupid," Gus said with disgust. "Feel better now? I'll get you a bandage and Tylenol but you'd better calm down. None of this drama is going to help you at all."

Leo dropped back face down on the mattress with his bleeding hand underneath his body. Who knows what kind of germs he might be picking up from that mattress, Gus thought. He'd better get some antiseptic too. There was a bottle of rubbing alcohol in the bathroom. He needed to put some in another container before taking it to Leo, who would undoubtedly drink the whole bottle, given the chance.

Gus went back to the house and tried to distract himself with video games but he couldn't settle down. He paced back and forth in the small living room, keeping an eye on the house across the driveway in case of trouble. Around noon, a beat-up Ford Fiesta drove up to his door and a skinny Anglo with long, stringy hair got out. Gus went outside to meet him.

"You Gus?"

"Yeah, who are you?"

"I'm Tony. Tucker sent me," he said. "Where's the patient?"

Gus closed the door and led Tony up the stairs and unlocked the door.

"Come get me when you're done with him so I can lock up again," Gus said. "I hope you can cool him out enough for him to stay quiet."

He left Tony alone with Leo and went down the stairs. His future with Julia depended on staying far away from whatever was going on up there.

L

Leo

Leo spent a miserable night on the dirty mattress. After a few hours of unconsciousness, he woke to find himself alone in the empty room. The sandwich he had not eaten was lying next to the mattress, covered in little black ants. He got to his feet and stumbled to the door. Locked. He had tried to call his father again, but it went straight to voicemail. His father must have turned off his phone. He vaguely remembered his conversation with the guy who locked him in, but couldn't seem to come up with the details.

How was he going to get out of here? Through the narrow barred windows on both ends of the room he could see that the street was deserted and there were no lights inside any of the buildings. The northside windows looked into the patio of a restaurant on the corner, now closed. Trees blocked his view of the street.

He crossed to the toilet, took a piss and dumped the ant-covered sandwich into the bucket of water before dumping the water in the tank to flush it. His brain fog cleared a bit and he remembered that his father said someone was coming with something, but he didn't expect that would happen before morning. He would have to tough out this night.

He flopped back down on the mattress clutching his stomach. The bad part of withdrawal was starting. Yesterday he had been restless and headachy but that was tolerable. What was coming would not be. Now his phone was dead, no way to call his dad or anyone else to rescue him.

The night passed slowly. Occasionally a police car or ambulance would come screaming by, responding to some Central Avenue early morning mayhem. Then there was total silence, not even a dog barked. When the sun finally came up, his patience was exhausted. The compound was still deserted. He started pounding on the door, hoping that it would awaken Gus. After a time, he heard Gus's footsteps hurrying across the driveway and up the stairs.

Later, after his hand was bandaged, Leo lay on his back on the mattress, staring at the ceiling and fantasizing about killing Ramon. That disgusting bean-eating puke, he should go back and get the gun he left in the tree trunk and blow his head off. He would go at night; it would be easy. But first he needed some drugs to level him out until he could get back in touch with his boys in Santa Fe who always had chiba and would trade for things Leo could steal, predominantly bicycles since his father had insisted that his mom come take her jewelry out of his house. Leo was enjoying thinking about how Ramon would look with his brains spattered on the wall of his trailer when a car drove up. He heard the car door slam, then the door of the house across the driveway. A few minutes later there were footsteps on the stairs, the door opened and sunshine poured in.

"I'm Tony. I hear you got some trouble."

Leo barely lifted his head off the mattress.

"You better have something for me," he growled. "I can't take much more of this gut pain."

"Got you some Oxys," Tony said. "But I can only give you two right now because I don't know how long you'll have to be here. It might be another day or two so I have to ration them."

Leo grabbed the water bottle from next to the mattress, the water was lukewarm. His hand shook has he took the tablets and tried to throw them into his mouth. One missed and landed on the floor near where a bunch of ants were attempting to carry away a piece of bread crust. Leo swept them away and grabbed the pill and swallowed it dry. He laid back down on the mattress.

Tony sat on the floor with his back to the door, waiting for the drugs to take effect so he could leave. He noticed there was a Mexican restaurant next door and he was hungry. He had spent the morning canvassing Belen for a few dozen Oxys; he knew most of the users in his hometown but not all of them were sellers. It had taken a few hours to find enough and then he had to drive up to Albuquerque.

But the money promised to be good, so he decided to treat himself to a good breakfast, then see what he could work out with the man in the house. Definitely a tight ass, he thought. No fun to be expected there. Maybe he would call that girl he met at his cousin's matanza a few months ago. They had been eyeing each other most of the evening and eventually started kissing behind the toolshed beyond the barbeque pit. They were definitely going to get busy except that his ride was leaving. What was her name? Adriana? Adria? He hoped he could get her number from his cousin. It looked like it was going to be a long day and night, no telling when someone would come and take this stupid kid off his hands.

Fortuna

Fortuna observed the arrival of the Anglo hippie. He was driving a beat-up car with cardboard taped over a missing back window. She watched him enter the house, then come out and cross the driveway. She heard him go up the stairs, then it was quiet. The people who lived in the houses on the south side had left in their cars hours before, nicely dressed and probably going to work. There had been a flurry of traffic along Rio Grande, probably other nine-to-five workers. After that, only the occasional car passed.

After the hippie came down and went back into the house, a young woman emerged from the inside stairwell leading to the upstairs apartments in the building across the driveway from where the men were coming and going. The Anglo woman was dressed in shorts, t-shirt and flip flops. She started to cross the parking lot to the mailboxes near the street, when another woman called to her from the balcony of the rear apartment.

"Ginny! If I throw down my key, will you check my mailbox too? The doctor says no stairs for me for at least another month."

This woman, also Anglo, was much older than the other one. Her hair was grey and she appeared to be leaning on a walker. The one called Ginny walked back to pick up the key thrown from the balcony into a flower box.

"I'm glad you caught me Milly," she said, nearly shouting as though the woman called Milly was hard of hearing. "I'm sorry you are stuck inside again. Jim and the baby and I are going camping for the weekend up north so we won't be around for a few days. It's been so hot we really need to get out of town and go someplace where it's cooler. Mandy has been pretty fussy. I think we all need some fresh air."

"I wish I could go with you," said Milly, "but it looks like I'm stuck here for a while longer."

As Ginny crossed to the mailboxes, both women appeared to see Fortuna, but neither seemed to pay her any mind. Tourists and others often spent time on that bench under the tree, getting out of the sun and checking their phones. But while they politely looked away, both women took note of what they assumed to be her race. Black people made up only two percent of the population in New Mexico, so they were unusual but did not inspire all the complicated feelings that surfaced in so many other places in the United States. Here the racial tension was more likely to be between Hispanos and Native Americans and the Anglos, which included Asians, Blacks and anyone else not indigenous to either Old or New Mexico.

On her way back from the mailboxes with her arms full of letters, magazines and flyers, Ginny nodded hello to Fortuna, who raised her good hand in greeting. An hour later, Ginny came down to her just-washed Honda carrying a baby in a car seat. Her husband followed with sleeping bags and a tent. While Ginny strapped the baby into the car, husband went back up for a large cooler. He didn't seem to pay any attention to Fortuna, but as their car pulled up next to her before turning onto the street, Ginny said something to him that caused him to glance at her surreptitiously. Fortuna was glad to see them drive away and considered that she might be becoming too conspicuous in this place too. Hopefully things would stay quiet until the workaday residents of the compound came home.

She took out *The Great Gatsby* and examined the cover illustration again. She hoped what was inside would be as interesting. While she turned to the first chapter, she watched the hippie emerge from the house and get into his car. As he exited the driveway, he looked hard at Fortuna with her suitcase, her hat and her book.

When he returned a half hour later, there was a blonde girl in the car with him and they both looked at Fortuna suspiciously. It was clear that the bench under the tree would be only a temporary refuge. When the complex's workers returned from work and found her still there, someone was bound to mention it.

"Too bad I have to find another place," she sighed. "But I also need to find a newspaper. Maybe the police have caught up with that young man. Maybe he is in jail or dead."

When it came to crime suspects, the police tended to shoot first. If he were dead, no one would be looking for her anymore. But she couldn't wish for that; she had started to realize that the boy reminded her of her grandson Billy, who was also slight and fair-skinned. And she had begun to fantasize about how she might help him. She missed Billy so much.

As the morning wore on it became uncomfortably hot, even in the shade of the tree. But there were storm clouds building to the north. It was monsoon season in New Mexico and violent afternoon downpours were common. The wind picked up, blowing dirt and leaves from the parking lot along the sidewalk. She could smell the rain coming and the tree that shaded her from the sun would be unlikely to shelter her from a storm.

As the first big drops started to fall, she stuffed her book into a side pocket of her suitcase and headed under the portal of the small apartment complex. Almost immediately the heavens opened and the rain came down in sheets. The wind blew the water towards her so that even under the portal, she was getting soaking wet. There were three steps up to a landing that led to the interior staircase where she had seen the young mother emerge early that morning. A metal gate barred the entrance, but when Fortuna pushed on it, it was not locked and swung open.

The stairway was well-lit by a series of lights embedded in the ceiling, one blinking on and off erratically like it was almost burned out. A dozen steps led up to two apartment doors. Fortuna put her suitcase down flat at the bottom of the stairs and climbed about halfway up to sit. From here, she would be invisible to anyone passing by the building. A person would have to enter the stairwell to see her, and she knew that the only resident at home was the elderly woman who could not climb the stairs.

"You must be watching over me, Ofelia. I will be out of the rain and out of sight. I can stay here until the family comes home on Sunday. I won't have to worry about the neighbors. They will think that I have moved on."

G

Gus

Gus wondered how the day could get any worse. He was angry that he had to miss work for the first time and irritated that Tony seemed to be planning to stay at the house while doling out drugs to Leo. He had been hopeful when Tony took out his car keys and headed for the door.

"So you'll come back tonight to check on the kid?" Gus said.

"Nah, I'll be right back," Tony said. "Just going to pick up a friend."

Shit, Gus thought. Rent free was more trouble than it was worth. Maybe he should start looking for his own place. He might have saved enough for a deposit and month's rent.

His thinking was further confirmed when Tony got back with his friend, a big blonde in cut-offs and a crop top, both a couple sizes too small for her ample and quite exposed flesh.

"Hi, I'm Desiree," she said, giving Gus a coy wave of her hand, glitter flashing from her long pink nails. "Got anything to drink? It's so hot out there."

"There are a few cokes in the refrigerator," Gus said. "I don't keep alcohol in the house."

"Mind if we go out and buy some beer?" asked Tony, seeing the look on Desiree's face. No alcohol was not going to work for her. Or for him, either, considering how long they were going to be there. The kid would be passed out or nearly so until evening and he didn't have enough money to take her to a bar all afternoon.

"You can't drink beer in the house," Gus said. "I can't be around it and I don't feel like staying in my room all day just so you can drink."

"Okay man, don't get excited," Tony said. "We'll drink it in the car."

Desiree didn't look too thrilled with this plan but she had faith in her ability to change a man's mind. She batted her eyes at Gus on her way out the door with Tony. But Gus was a man in love so he was immune. No way are they drinking in the house, he thought. I may have to lock them out.

To his surprise, they didn't ask to come in, except to use the bathroom. Once she had a couple of beers, Desiree didn't mind about the car. She and Tony also split one of the Oxys Tony was holding for Leo, figuring the kid was too far gone to be able to say how many he took. Tony and Desiree passed the afternoon in a drowsy haze, occasionally rousing themselves to grope each other a bit before losing interest and nodding off again. But by evening, the effects of the drug wore off, leaving them with just headaches from the beer and the heat. Dark storm clouds were moving in and distant thunder and lightning suggested another monsoon deluge.

"Let's get out of here and go somewhere," Desiree said. "We could take a drive to the Tiki Bar down on Central, it's not that far. I want to drink something else. I'm tired of beer, I want a margarita."

Tony went up to check on Leo, who was still lethargic and fuzzy but was able to get down another Oxycontin, so Tony wouldn't have to worry about him for a few more hours. As he was coming down the stairs, the heavens opened and it started to pour. The car would no longer be a good place to be since the water came pouring in around the edges of the cardboard in the broken window. Since they had consumed all the beer, Tony figured Gus would let them in the house. He knocked before opening the door, but Gus wasn't in the living room. Tony figured maybe he had gone to bed and beckoned for Desiree to come inside.

Actually, Gus was in his room composing a long email to Julia while the rain hammered on the tin roof of the house. He heard Tony come in, then heard Desiree laugh. He came into the living room where they were together on the couch. Desiree lay on top of Tony, who had his hand down the back of her shorts.

"No booze in the house, I hope," Gus said.

"Nah, we finished it in the car," Tony said. "I checked on the kid, gave him another pill and he went back to sleep. It's pouring outside and the car leaks so I hope it's okay if we come inside."

Gus was so tired of the whole situation—the strung out kid, these scuzzy caretakers with a beater car sitting in his driveway—he didn't want to think about it anymore.

"Okay, you can stay inside," he said. "But no more beer or drugs and no more company. You can get some food at Sofia's on the corner or there's some leftover pizza in the fridge. I'm going to bed."

He was glad his room was far enough back down the hall that he wouldn't have to hear whatever other activities they were liable to get into. He wished he had put some towels or sheets on the couch and he wasn't thinking about the rainwater.

Hours later, Gus was awakened by a loud crash, followed by the beeping of a car horn that seemed to be stuck. There was shouting outside the house. He looked at the bedside clock: three am. He pulled on some jeans and ran out into the living room where Tony was passed out on the couch. He heard a woman screaming outside. He turned on the outside light and opened the door. Tony's car had crashed into the side of Rumaldo's house, tearing through some of the bushes, ripping off an outside water spigot and damaging the gas line into the house. Desiree stood by the car's open door hollering and bleeding from a gash on her forehead.

"Help me, help me." She swayed unsteadily on her feet and directed her pleas to the building across the parking lot where some lights had come on following the crash. Gus knew those people would not be coming down to such a scene. But someone evidently did call the police because ten minutes later a squad car showed up. Soon there were three police cars blocking the entrance to the parking lot. Two officers cornered Desiree, who tried to retreat to the house. Another disabled the car horn. Tony, finally roused from his deep sleep, came outside and stood with Gus.

"What the fuck, man," said Gus.

"I didn't have money to take her out, I guess she got mad and tried to leave."

"Don't we have enough problems here already?" said Gus with disgust. Since getting sober, he had no sympathy for this sort of drama. He glanced up uneasily to the windows of the blockhouse, hoping Leo was sufficiently drugged to not complicate matters further. He caught a glimpse of Leo's pale face in the window and motioned for him to get back to where he could not be seen.

One of the cops came over to where Gus and Tony were standing.

"Whose car is this?" he asked.

"It's mine," Tony said.

"Was she driving it with your permission? She appears to be intoxicated," said the cop.

"I was asleep," Tony said. "She must have taken the keys from my pocket."

Another officer finished his inventory of the contents of the car, noting the twenty-four empty beer cans. He took some pictures. The first cop had finished giving Desiree the standard field sobriety test, which she failed.

"We're going to have to take her in," he said to Tony. "If you can drive your car, get it out of there."

" We'll have to notify the gas company and the owner of the building," he said to Gus. "He'll want to get the insurance guys out here ASAP. She took a pretty good chunk out of the wall. We'll get the gas shut off immediately but they'll have to inspect the house before anyone can go in."

Tony walked towards the car, trying to catch Desiree's eye. She was sitting on the ground by the wall with her head in her hands. She didn't look up. Tony was able to back the car away from the wall and drive it back into the space between the two houses.

The cops stayed for another hour, talking and laughing amongst themselves, the red lights still flashing on all the cars, preventing anyone already awake in the complex from getting back to sleep. Finally they put Desiree in one of the squad cars, switched off the lights and headed out. Suddenly it was very dark and quiet. Out of the shadows, Gus saw Rod walking across the parking lot from the art gallery.

"A little excitement tonight," he said.

"Sorry if it woke you up," said Gus. "I'm glad she didn't run into one of your cars," he said, indicating the shiny sedans parked by the gallery entrance. None of them belonged to Rod, but he said nothing.

Gus knew he would have to get Leo out of the building before morning or he would surely be discovered but he couldn't have him in his house. Maybe he could stay in Tony's car until his dad could figure out somewhere else for him to hide out. But Tony had other ideas.

"I've got to go check on her," Tony said. "I don't have any money to bail her out but I told her we could go downtown but then I passed out. I feel responsible."

Actually, he was afraid Desiree might mention the Oxys they were taking and implicate him in something bigger than a DWI. If he could talk to her he could tell her about his lawyer friend who could get her out for free. He had seen it work before, but it was going to take a little time to work out. He held out the bottle of pills that Leo's dad paid for, trying to give it to Gus.

"Two of these Oxys will knock him out for twelve hours or so," he said. "Just keep dosing him until somebody can come and take him home."

Gus stepped back and held up his hands.

"I can't take those and I won't be responsible for giving them to him," he said. "I'm not going to jeopardize my sobriety. I just won't do it. I told my uncle that when he sent the kid here and he said I wouldn't have to be involved with any drugs."

Tony pivoted and handed the bottle to Rod instead.

"You guys work it out," he said. "I'm out of here."

Tony got into his badly damaged car and headed out the driveway. The car was missing a headlight and was making a scraping noise. He got out and pulled the front fender away from the tire, then drove off.

Rod looked at the bottle. Oxycontin, damn. He loved those. It would make the long hours in the gallery more enjoyable, for sure.

"What's the story?" he asked Gus. Gus knew he was taking a risk telling this stranger what was going on, but he was desperate and Rod seemed sympathetic. He decided to take that chance.

"There's a kid up in that blockhouse who's wanted by the cops," he said. "He's all strung out on smack and his father got Tony to bring those pills to keep him quiet until they can get him back to Santa Fe. I'm in recovery and I can't be around this stuff. I'm already way too involved. Plus I have to get him out of that building before the inspectors come. They will want to look up there."

Rod put on his most sympathetic expression. This could work out well for him.

"You're in a spot," he said. "I have some experience with this. I'm in recovery from heroin addiction myself." This was a lie, but he could tell it was having the desired effect on Gus.

"There's a back room behind the gallery with a bed," he said. "He can stay there for a while. There's not too much traffic through the gallery on the weekends."

There was not much traffic there at any time, but Gus was gone all day so he would not have noticed that. Rod didn't sleep in the bedroom himself so he didn't mind giving it up to Leo. He could easily find the kid some smack and keep the Oxys for himself.

Gus agreed to the plan. He saw little alternative.

Fortuna

Fortuna watched the police drama unfold from her perch in the stairwell. She had been asleep when the car hit the wall just opposite where she was sitting. It was hard to imagine how it happened, as the wall was a good five feet from the driveway. When the girl started screaming for help, it was pretty clear that she was intoxicated.

The noise from the car horn was loud and insistent.

"Someone will call the police. I'll have to move farther up the stairs to stay out of sight."

Sure enough, the police soon arrived but to her relief, they showed no interest in her building. They sat the girl down on the bench where Fortuna had spent the day. She considered that the universe may have sent the storm to remove her from a place where she would have been discovered and deposited her in a safe harbor.

She watched the two men outside the house across the way. After the cops had thrown all the beer cans out of the car, the hippie inspected the car and after a few adjustments was able to drive it back into the parking space in front of the house. Fortuna would have liked to go back to sleep but the cops stayed around until nearly dawn. They took the girl with them.

After the cops left, Fortuna watched a third man come out of the gallery downstairs and cross the driveway to talk with the men. She had not seen him before. He was a tall Anglo, probably handsome once but going to seed. She watched him interact with the other men,

"That one can't be trusted, she said to Ofelia. "He's not like the young man who lives in the house. His face I like. That one is like my nephews, the good ones. The older one looks like he is hiding something,"

She couldn't hear all of the conversation but she observed the passing of a container which she assumed were drugs. She watched the nice one refuse to take it from the hippie and how the gallery man had taken it. The hippie got in his car and drove away, while the other two men talked briefly. Then the nice one took the other one under the stairs to the blockhouse to retrieve a key from under a flowerpot, then went back into his house. The other man went up to the room at the top of the stairs.

Fortuna's mind was racing. These events were so strange and the night, now so quiet, made her thoughts wander to what a possible explanation might be. This was one effect of her passion for books. She loved a good story and couldn't help constructing one from unusual happenings.

As she was wondering about what she had seen earlier, she watched the gallery man come down the stairs, followed by a boy. As they crossed the driveway, an outside light shone on the boy's face, which made her gasp and catch her breath. It was the boy from the river, still in his black t-shirt. Why was he here and where was he going? She realized suddenly what had been nagging at her since she saw his face the first time.

"He looks like Billy," she whispered.

They were both slight with sandy hair and pale skin. The boy looked unwell and her heart went out to him. She had an instinct to protect him, to warn him about the man from the gallery. But she could not give her presence away without jeopardizing her hiding place. And what did she have to offer the boy? She had nothing for herself, much less anything to share. She watched the man and the boy walk under the portal, then heard the door to the gallery close behind them. The quiet returned. She unzipped her suitcase and made sure Diego's gun was still wrapped up in a shawl at the bottom. She piled the books on top and zipped it back up.

The sun was almost up so Fortuna left her suitcase near the top of the stairs and walked across the street to the public bathroom off the Plaza. She quickly relieved herself and washed up as much as possible in the sink, grabbing a handful of paper towels, one to dry herself and the others she stuffed into the top of her dress for later use. Hurrying back to the street, she saw the nice man from across the driveway come out of his house and lock the door. He crossed to the gallery and peered in the windows but soon walked away, headed towards Central Avenue. She assumed he would be gone all day. She watched him leave and waited until he was halfway down the block before crossing the street and ducking into the stairwell.

"I hope I can stay here until that family comes home tomorrow," she said. "I can't get too comfortable in case they get caught in the rains and come home early."

After she caught her breath, she unzipped her suitcase and took out *The Great Gatsby.* She chose it partly because it was dog-eared and well worn, which meant it had been read many times. She knew it would be about things as foreign to her experience as the scene on the book's cover, the blond man gazing at the green light. She took an apple and a box of crackers from the suitcase, supplies left over from her last visit to the food pantry downtown. Soon she was lost in the world of very rich people who lived on the water in New York and despite their wealth, were still unhappy. She was a little ashamed to note how this cheered her. She knew money didn't buy happiness but she was always glad to have her belief confirmed by such stories.

After she had read a few chapters, she heard the gallery door open and the man who she had disliked on sight came out and walked to the street and turned the corner.

"I'm worried about the boy, maybe I should go down and see if he's alright, He looked so sick"

Since the gallery was presumably open to the public, maybe she could go see, but she decided it was too risky. These people were hiding him from the police, that was obvious. Better to not get involved. Less than an hour later, the man came back. A few minutes later a loud car pulled into the driveway and passed Fortuna's line of sight before stopping outside the gallery. The door opened and closed briefly, then the driver came out and roared off. The gallery guy went back inside and she heard him turn both of the locks on the door. Then it was quiet again.

She must have become drowsy and leaned back against the stairs, lifting her feet from where they rested on the suitcase. She was startled awake by the sound of the suitcase bumping down the stairs, landing with a thud on the landing below. She sat up and intended to go after it when she heard a door open above her.

"Hello?" said the elderly woman peering out the door, her path blocked by her walker.

"I'm sorry for the noise," said Fortuna. "I fell asleep."

The two woman looked at each other for a long minute. The one at the door—Milly, the younger woman had called her—nodded at Fortuna. Then she closed the door.

"Is she going to call the police? She didn't ask any questions. Something in her eyes. I think she is sorry for me. Maybe she will let me be."

Fortuna knew she would have to leave when the family came home. They would want to protect their child from a homeless person squatting outside their door. But maybe she would be safe until then.

Leo

Leo couldn't tell how long he had been knocked out when the older man shook him awake. He was still lying on the dirty mattress in the empty room but it seemed to be getting light outside.

"C'mon kid, we gotta get you out of here," the man said. "There's been an accident and the cops were here. They'll be back."

"Who are you?" said Leo.

"I'm Rod, I've got the gallery in that building across the driveway. You're gonna stay with me for a while, at least until the cops stop buzzing around."

"Where's that other guy? Tony," Leo said, sitting up and quickly laying back down. "I'm sick. He has something I need."

"Yeah I know all about it," Rod said. "Tony's gone. I'm gonna get you what you want. You won't have to take those pills that make you sleep around the clock."

"You're kidding," said Leo. "That's what I want to hear. Let's go."

Rod helped him get to his feet. He swayed and hung onto Rod's arm while he tried to focus his eyes.

"Are you going to be able to get down the stairs?" Rod asked.

"Yeah yeah, I'll just hold onto the railing," Leo said. "I need to go slow."

Leo descended the stairs behind Rod, his anticipation of getting high seeming to improve his walking ability. They crossed the parking lot as the sky in the east was glowing pink behind the Sandia mountains visible above and beyond the roofs of Old Town. Leo was unaware of his surroundings, but focused on the promise of a real fix instead of the pills that made him feel dopey.

The two men walked under the portal to the gallery entrance and went inside. Rod's futon and blankets were still on the floor in the front room, in which a dozen paintings of various sizes decorated the walls. Rod led Leo to a room in the back, which contained a real bed but no windows.

"Stay here," Rod said. "I have to go out to find you some H. I will lock the door. If anyone knocks, just stay in the back."

"Got anything to drink?" asked Leo.

Rod crossed to a small refrigerator in the corner.

"Beer? Coke?"

"Yeah I'll take a coke," Leo said. He chugged it, sat down on the bed and burped. He felt the sugar entering his blood and the pain in his stomach subsided a bit. He lay back and closed his eyes. Rod closed the bedroom door and soon afterwards, Leo heard him go out the front door and lock it behind him.

Leo thought he should tell his father where he had gone, but his phone was still dead. He went out into the gallery space, looking for a landline phone, which he supposed every business had, but he found nothing. He began idly opening drawers in the desk that faced the door. The bottom drawer was locked, but Leo was an expert lock picker. A little turn with a letter opener lying on the desk did the trick. The drawer was filled with cash. Fifties and one hundreds, and a few twenties. He could buy plenty of chiba with that. He blinked hard and tried to think. Was this the time to make a break for it? He felt weak, his head and stomach hurt and except for Ramon, he had no idea where to look for a fix. Ramon was not an option. He could call an Uber to take him to Santa Fe but his phone was dead. There was a phone charger plugged into the wall but it wouldn't fit into his phone. He closed the drawer and went to the back room and lay down on the bed. Rod was going to take care of him, there would be time enough to grab some cash before he left town.

Some minutes later, he heard Rod come back but his hopes for a quick fix were deflated. Rod stood in the doorway emptyhanded.

"Sorry, we had to send out for it," Rod said. "The guy I work for usually has some but he was out. Don't worry, it won't be too long. Want another coke?"

Leo felt his anger rising. Maybe he should just grab some of that cash and get out of here. He could figure out the details later. Rod would have to use the bathroom eventually, he just needed a few minutes alone and he could be gone. As he was hatching this plan, he heard the noise of a car coming down the driveway. Rod went to the door and let someone in. They exchanged a few words, then Rod crossed the room to the desk.

After a quiet minute or two, a drawer opened, then closed. Leo held his breath, he had to leave the drawer unlocked since he had no key. The door opened and closed again and he heard the motorcycle depart.

Rod was standing in the doorway again, holding a paper packet. He tossed it on the bed next to Leo.

"Sorry dude, couldn't put my hands on any works for you," Rod said. "You'll have to snort it for now, there's more where that came from."

Leo's hands were shaking as he unfolded the paper and bent to inhale some. He was so focused on the drugs that he didn't notice that Rod was looking at him suspiciously.

Rod

The kid was messed up, Rod thought. But maybe not too messed up to snoop around the gallery. He never left that drawer unlocked, no matter how wrecked he might get after a big cash transaction. He would either have to count it all again or take a look in the kid's pockets after he passed out, obviously the easier choice.

He had asked Juan, the dealer who lived around the corner, for some proper works for the kid so he could really knock himself out. It might be easier to search him then. Rod and Juan worked for the same guy, who they seldom saw. He was a big man who spoke with an accent, probably Mexican. Rod had watched *Breaking* Bad like everyone else in New Mexico. The guy seemed dangerous and Rod avoided him whenever possible.

It was Sal from the casino. who had gotten him his present job after he was fired. One night an acquaintance from Taos had talked him into help him cheat at blackjack.

"It'll be easy, it's foolproof," the man said." Just use the deck I give you and I'll cut you in."

It had seemed like a good idea at the time, but Rod had been doing a lot of coke that week and it quickly became obvious to the other players that something was off. A complaint to the manager shut down the game and Rod was put on leave, Then the incident triggered a drug test, which he had no time to doctor. So the casino gig was over like all the other gigs, ignominiously enough that he could count on no references.

But after collecting his final paycheck and heading for the parking lot, Sal had called out to him. He didn't really know Sal, he was just one of the characters who roamed the casino. Because he had an Italian name and liked shiny suits and big rings, Rod had assumed he was a part of the mob. Which mob exactly he wasn't sure, but he figured the Mafia would be interested in Indian casinos. They seemed like an easy way to launder money, something else Rod didn't know much about.

"I know some guys in Albuquerque who might have a job for you," he said. "Easy money and no one will care if you're using."

Rod took the referral, vague as it was. He drove to Santa Fe the next day to meet with one of Sal's friends, who told him about the gallery job. It sounded easy enough, so easy it was probably not entirely legal. But Rod didn't know what was going on with this gallery and preferred to remain ignorant of the details. He would have deniability if the worst should happen. The fact that he knew nothing about art didn't seem to be a problem.

When he first saw where he would be working, his suspicions seemed to be confirmed. The gallery was well back from the street and although it was technically in Old Town, it was not on any walking route. It was clear that the clientele would be people who knew to come there.

Sal sent him to a house on the very narrow and curiously named Hollywood Street, around the corner from the gallery. The house was two-story with a wide ground floor porch under a portal and a dirt yard where you could park a dozen cars. There was a locked gate at the street entrance and a low adobe wall separated the property from a narrow deserted lot.

Rod noticed that none of the houses on the other side of the vacant lot had windows on that side. He figured the unsightly lot must have been there when the houses were built, but they were not new. It was strange, he thought, but pretty convenient for whatever business was being conducted in the house. There were few places with a view into the yard, although there was one balcony on the second floor of the gallery building.

A young kid who didn't speak English had opened the gate for Rod. An enormous dog was chained up under the portal and barked furiously at Rod, who stayed a good distance away. He did not like dogs of any kind and certainly not this monster. This was the kind of dog that people poisoned, he thought. If he lived here, he might do it himself. There were several other cars in the yard, including a shiny black Escalade. The kid beckoned for him to come into the house where there seemed to be a party going on. Rod could hear the music when he drove in. Something about taking a horse to Old Town Road. Well this wasn't what he expected of Old Town. He thought it would be more...classy.

"Can't nobody tell me nothin'," the song went on. Rod straightened his spine and let the kid take him into the house. Inside it was dimly lit but Rod could see lights in the kitchen in the back, where three men were sitting around a table. As he passed through the darkened living room he saw two women sprawled across the couches. They were scantily dressed but not young and what Rod would have called skanky not too long ago. But along with his fortunes, his standards had fallen of late. He'd had worse-looking one night stands, you just don't turn on the lights. But for now, he followed the kid to the kitchen. The men at the table, who were counting large stacks of bills, looked up.

"I'm Rod. Sal sent me. About the gallery position."

The men laughed. One stood up and extended his hand.

"I'm Juan," he said. "Have a seat. Let me finish this and I'll take you over there. The boss may want to buy a painting."

The other men laughed again.

Rod sat on the only empty chair, but pushed it back from the table a bit. He didn't want to appear too comfortable sitting so close to stacks of cash. He noticed that two of the men had big guns stuffed into the waistbands of their jeans.

"Do you have any experience dealing art?" asked Juan. "Or running a business?"

"I have a degree in business," Rod said, "but no, I never operated one. Sal thought I could handle this one."

The men laughed again. Rod was pretty sure they all knew something he didn't about this art gallery gig. But he decided not to attempt to get any more information. Questions didn't seem like they would be welcomed here. He waited for the men to finish their counting. They bound the stacks of bills with rubber bands and put all of it in a gym bag. All of the men except Juan got up and went into the living room and sat down to grope the women, who made weak and unconvincing protests.

As Juan and Rod prepared to leave with the gym bag, a tall man with a large head came down the stairs from the upper floor. Rod noted that he wore an expensive suit and had small, mean eyes. Juan nodded at him but the man ignored both of them. He was followed by a tall, dark-skinned woman, this one much more attractive than the others. Rod tried to catch her eye but she was expressionless and didn't seem to see him. Her eyes were glassy and Rod noticed angry red marks on her neck. The big man headed for the door and one of the gropers on the couch sprang up to open it for him. They both went outside and as Rod and Juan exited, they saw the young boy open the gate for the departing Escalade.

"We can take my car," Rod said.

"No," said Juan. "You leave the car here, you won't need it."

"I've got a few things I need to take," Rod said. He retrieved his back pack from the passenger seat of the Fiat. It contained a change of clothes and a toothbrush and razor, enough for a couple of days but eventually he would need to get more of his belongings from the apartment in Pojoaque. He needed to find a place in Albuquerque, he decided. It was too long a drive for him to commute.

Rod followed Juan around the corner to the gallery. They walked up the breezeway and past a low landing leading to a stairway to the upstairs apartments. Juan unlocked the door and Rod followed him inside.

The front room had paintings both on and stacked against the wall. Rod didn't know much about art but they seemed similar and unimpressive, mostly landscapes and abstracts. There was a desk and chair in one corner. An older model desktop computer sat on one side. Juan opened the bottom drawer of the desk and dumped in the contents of the gym bag. From another drawer he withdrew a receipt book and called Rod over to watch him fill it out. Juan listed three landscapes and an abstract, with prices adding up to forty thousand dollars.

"In a couple of days, someone will come by and take the cash to the bank," Juan said. "I'll call you to say when. In the meantime, just mind the store. If someone comes in and wants to buy a painting, you can negotiate a lower price than we put on these four," he said, gesturing to the ones he had just purchased. "This needs to look like a regular business to anyone who comes in off the street. When the boss wants to make a purchase like tonight, I'll contact you. The boss likes to do business at night so it could be late. Otherwise, you can just hang here. There's a bedroom and bathroom in the back and a small kitchen. There's some beer in the refrigerator, just let me know what else you need. All the restaurants around here will deliver, you can find their websites on the computer."

Rod was getting the picture that he was going to be pretty well trapped in this place. What had he gotten himself into? Time to back out and come up with another plan.

"I'm not sure I'm the best man for this job," he said. "I don't know anything about art or running an art gallery."

Juan's face was stern.

"Sal should have made something clear: you are part of the organization now," he said. "We don't know you nearly well enough to allow you to quit. When we know we can trust you, we can talk about your role."

Juan opened the drawer and counted out a thousand dollars, which he handed to Rod.

"First week's salary," he said. "Just be cool and everything will work out." He locked the drawer and handed the key to Rod. He picked up the four paintings and opened the door. "I'll be back tomorrow.'

Rod was liking this less and less. He wished he had some good drugs and maybe one of those women from Juan's house to help get him through the night. He took his backpack into the bedroom and dropped it on the bed. The room was claustrophobic, a low ceiling and no windows. There was a futon in one corner and he dragged the mattress out into the gallery space. At least there was some light coming in from the streetlights. Maybe he could find some porn to watch on the computer.

Over the next few weeks, he learned a few other coping mechanisms for the tedium of days at the gallery. Beer and masturbating to pornography on TV were major occupations. He also spent a fair amount of time revisiting a few of his conquests from the casinos. That one with the Kim Kardashian butt. He could come just looking at it. Better than looking at her face, which showed her age. She did give a great blow job and he didn't have to look at her wrinkles.

Occasionally he would be called to close the gallery and walk over to the house on Hollywood where Juan and his boys lived. Sometimes there were girls around and there were always drugs. Most of the regulars at the house were heroin fans and that was always on offer. Rod had tried it once and got sick so it ceased to be of any interest. He preferred cocaine and got some from Juan the first week but it didn't go well with his new lifestyle. He became too agitated to just sit in the gallery or outside on the breezeway. He started pacing and got some curious looks from neighbors. Finally he persuaded Juan to bring him a bottle of Jack, which leveled him out a bit. After that, he was typically on the hunt for Valium, which was helpful. Oxys would be better but no one at the house on Hollywood were into those.

So by the time Desiree crashed Tony's car into the wall, Rod was ready for some drama in his life. Access to his drug of choice just sealed the deal. It was easy enough to get the kid some horse in exchange.

He made a quick trip to the house on Hollywood. Only Juan was there and he was tapped out but he promised to send over a connection soon. Rod didn't tell him that it wasn't for him, he assumed taking in the kid wouldn't be approved by Juan or by the boss. Rod had seen him again twice at the house, always coming or going from upstairs, where Rod had never been. He had not seen the pretty girl again.

Now, he would wait to make sure Leo was crashed out in the bedroom before sampling his pills. He knew his pills well enough to realize they were not from a pharmacy. They lacked the coding stamped on every real Oxycontin. But Rod knew guys up north who could duplicate the formula pretty well. He had never been a careful man and was unlikely to start now.

He checked on Leo who was sprawled out on his back. He looked pretty bad, Rod thought. Hopefully someone would come get him before too long. But he had asked Juan for a little more heroin and a syringe, just in case.

As Rod came out of the bedroom, there was a knock at the door.

"Door's open!"

Gus poked his head in.

"Sorry I wasn't sure you were doing business today," he said. Truthfully the gallery never seemed to be doing any business. "How is the patient?"

"He's asleep," Rod said. "Took one of his magic pills and floated off to dreamland. Is someone coming to get him? He's not in great shape and if he takes these pills every six hours they won't last long."

"I will try to get a message to his father," Gus said.

"What's his story, anyway?' said Rod. "Who's he hiding from?"

"I don't have a lot of information," Gus said. "My uncle works for his father. He asked us to help him lay low for a while. It doesn't help that he's so strung out."

"Well anyway, let me know when he might be leaving," Rod said. He didn't tell Gus that he suspected Leo of breaking into the desk drawer where the cash was kept. But the sooner the kid was gone, the better. As soon as Gus left and crossed the parking lot to his house, Rod grabbed a beer from his refrigerator, took the pill bottle out of his pocket and downed one.

Juan

Juan grew up in a tiny village in the northern New Mexico mountains that was for a time the heroin capital of the Southwest. Heroin was everywhere when he was growing up, but Juan was determined to avoid it. His parents were hard-working, God-fearing people who tried to ignore the drug scourge right in their backyard.

Juan went to school down in the valley and he worked hard to keep his grades up. He found a sympathetic math teacher who helped him navigate the dangerous shoals of high school. He joined the mariachi band and went to mariachi festivals in other southwestern cities, broadening his formerly narrow horizons. His mentor helped him apply to community college to study computer science.

By this time, his younger brother had become ensnared in the Chimayo drug world and Juan's home became a place of anger, fights and sorrow. Most nights, he stayed in the college library until it closed. After graduation, he used his mentor again to get an internship at INTEL and despite his mother's tears, he moved to Albuquerque to start his new life.

Juan loved the big city and he loved INTEL, where he eventually landed a fulltime job.

"Everyone is smart and serious, but we go out and grab lunch once in a while so I'm feeling much more comfortable," he told Steve and Ray, some friends he met in college before they dropped out. They invited him to share their house in Old Town, close to where they worked at a big hotel. Juan had been living in a shabby studio so he agreed.

Juan knew that neither of them were as ambitious as he was and that they drank a lot, probably did a lot more than that. But it was fun to live in Old Town, close to the museums and parks. He was saving money for a down payment on a house but kept his dream a secret. He didn't want other people asking questions, the dream was just for him. He let it run free in his mind only in bed, before sleep.

One winter night during Juan's second year in Albuquerque, he awoke to the sound of gunshots outside the house. He called out for his roommates but they were both outside in the driveway, where he could hear a car peeling out. Lights were going on in all the surrounding houses; someone would have called the police by now. As Ray pushed past Juan into the house, he was holding what looked like a handgun.

Steve was up at the street when the police car arrived. Juan started walking up the driveway along with a few other neighbors, most wearing coats over pajamas.

A white car was blocking the driveway, all four doors open and nobody inside. A variety of men's tennis shoes were scattered around inside and outside of the car. One of the neighbors whose apartment faced Rio Grande had heard some of the fight that preceded the shooting. He said it seemed to be about fake designer shoes.

Juan stood under the portal, close enough to listen to the police question everyone, starting with Steve, who was yelling at the cops that his buddy's car had been stolen. After listening to the upstairs neighbors account, Juan put together that the thieves arrived in the white car, which had been stolen an hour before. Ray had been on his way out of the driveway in his red Firebird when the dissatisfied customers spotted him.

They pulled in and started throwing shoes at Ray, who sprinted back to his house, where he grabbed a gun and went back outside to confront his attackers who by this time were sitting in the Firebird. Ray got off four fairly random shots for scare effect, not really wanting to damage his car. When they heard the police siren coming down Central Avenue, the bangers peeled out and disappeared up the street.

Eventually the landlord arrived from his opulent house across town.

"Anyone in this complex have a home security cam or a doorbell camera?" the cop asked the landlord.

"Actually yes," the landlord said. "The house these guys live in has a doorbell cam."

The landlord and the cop walked back down the driveway to what Juan was already thinking of as his former house. They knocked on the door and Ray answered. By the time Juan arrived, the cop and the landlord were sitting in the living room with Steve and Ray and there were grim faces all around.

"Did *you* erase it?" the landlord asked as soon as he walked in.

"Erase what?"

"The doorbell cam video."

"No, I wouldn't know how to do that."

Apparently, everyone was denying it. Not long afterward, some news vans showed up and parked a block away. Some cameramen filmed the white car until it was towed away. It became a local news story for a minute, but it was unsavory enough that they were evicted from the house.

Steve and Ray didn't much care. They had plenty of leisure time to find another apartment in the neighborhood. But Juan had been working as much overtime as possible and needed a place to stay until things slowed down.

Juan sat on his dresser in the driveway outside of the house, waiting for a friend to come take his few pieces of furniture to a storage locker. A familiar face in a Lobos hat ran past the driveway and Juan called to him.

"Hey Dave, you know of anyone around here who needs a roommate?"

Dave slowed down and began walking down the driveway.

"What's going on, man? You moving?"

"Not exactly voluntarily," Juan said. "One of my roommates was playing with a gun outside and then he erased the doorbell camera footage."

"Oh wow, sorry man," Dave said. "I guess I did hear those shots a few nights ago. I just figured it's Old Town, always some kids screwing around."

Dave stood thinking for a moment,

"Hey if you need a place to stay, you could help me out. I'm staying around the corner on Hollywood," he said. "There's a dog and everyone living there is gone for a few days. If you want to stay at the house and feed the dog, I can go check on some family things up north. Could work out for both of us."

Juan didn't see too many options so he accepted. He wasn't committing to much, just a couple of days. After he had disposed of his furniture, he jumped the fence over by the garbage cans and walked across the vacant lot and over the low adobe wall of the big house. Dave met him at the door and showed him to a small bedroom on the ground floor.

"You can leave your things here," Dave said. "No need to go upstairs.

I'll show you around the kitchen and where you can find the dogfood. That's all you'll need."

Juan was grateful for a few extra days to find another place to live, but he couldn't resist having a look around the house after Dave left. There were several bedrooms upstairs and a balcony that faced east. A nice place to watch the sunrise, Juan thought. There was a closed-in feeling about the downstairs, dark with too much overstuffed furniture. He was sorry he hadn't asked Dave if he could sleep upstairs. Maybe he would do that anyway, there was no one else around.

For the next few days, he returned to the house after work, fed the dog, ate some fast food he picked up on the way home, then took advantage of the quiet and solitude to go to bed early.

Looking for an extra blanket when it turned cold, he discovered why he was not supposed to go upstairs. The closet in the room where he had been sleeping was filled with bricks of white powder. Juan didn't know what it was exactly but he had a few good guesses. Suddenly, it didn't seem so advantageous to be staying at this house. He packed up his few things and was preparing to jump the wall back to the vacant lot and then the street, when Dave drove back into the yard.

He slammed the door of his car.

"Where you going?" he said.

"I've decided to go back up north where my family is," Juan said. "I think Albuquerque is too much city for me."

Dave wasn't buying it.

"Come back into the house," he said. "I have to give you some information that you need."

Juan looked at him warily. He wished he had been able to get away before Dave arrived. He didn't want to be rude, but he wanted to be away from there.

He followed Dave back into the house and stopped inside the front door. Dave thought for a moment, then walked up the stairs, down the hall, where he stopped for a minute, then back down the stairs.

"You stayed upstairs," he said. "I wish you hadn't done that."

"It's light up there," Juan said, "and I liked the view."

"Look, Juan, I saw how you were hurrying away and you didn't call me to say you were leaving," Dave said. "I'm going to assume that you know what goes on in this house when they are in business. I'm sorry you got a little nosy, but I'm afraid you're doing to have to become part of this operation until they know they can trust you or until they shut down at this location."

"Oh no, man, the last thing I want is to have anything to do with a drug organization," Juan said. "I'm in school and I work at INTEL."

"I'll talk to the boss about you," Dave said, "that's the best I can do. You'll have to stay here and we'll find a spot for you."

So Dave moved back in to keep an eye on Juan until the other men returned from Mexico. Juan stayed at the house, biding his time and hoping to gain enough of the boss's trust that he might be able to escape and disappear into the mountains.

Because he was smart and good with numbers, he was soon responsible for the money. The runners would bring their cash back to the house and the kitchen guys would count it under Juan's supervision. Juan knew of a ground-floor space near where he used to live, and Dave rented it to house an art gallery. The boss would use it to launder the money they took in until it came time to leave and set up in another city.

F

Fortuna

Fortuna was grateful for the shade in the stairwell and for protection from the hot wind that was blowing all day. It was not terribly comfortable sitting on the concrete stairs but she took a coat out of the suitcase to sit on. She saw a few bugs crawling in and out of the cracks in the plaster on the opposite wall, but they kept their distance. A number of cars went by, headed for the houses further down the driveway, and a man in a car parked and appeared to go into the gallery. But despite the lights that burned all night, she finally managed to drop off to sleep. When she awoke in the early morning, she could see a trace of pink in the sky to the east.

Once again, she left her things in the stairwell and crossed the street to use the public bathroom at the entrance to the Plaza. This time she dragged the suitcase all the way up to the landing so it would look like it belonged to someone who lived there. And before she left it, she made sure that the gun was tied up in the flannel shirt she had been wearing before it got hot.

"I don't think the disabled viejita will come out and open it," she told Ofelia "But I need to be sure. It will be so much faster to leave it here,"

When she returned to her hideout, the street was still empty of both cars and people but she heard the bell at the church on the Plaza calling the faithful to worship. Fortuna would not be among them.

"I have asked God for mercy for many years and waited patiently for him to hear me," she told Ofelia. "I'm sorry Abuela. I try hard to still believe but I don't worship."

Walking into the stairwell, she saw something placed on top of the suitcase at the top of the stairs. When she was close enough, she saw it was a large burrito on a plate. She touched it with a finger: it was still warm. It must be from the old lady from yesterday.

As much as she appreciated the food, she felt exposed and vulnerable and bumped the suitcase halfway down the stairs before sitting down next to it and biting into the burrito. It was delicious. Scrambled eggs, bacon, potatoes and cheese and just a little chile, exactly the way she liked it. It was gone in minutes. Fortuna leaned against the wall and closed her eyes, savoring the closest thing to a hot meal she had enjoyed in days. A while later, as she had hoped and expected, the door to the upstairs apartment opened and the woman called Milly came out onto the landing, leaning on a cane.

"Le gusto?" she asked.

"Si, si," said Fortuna. "Me gusto mucho, gracias." She rose and climbed up a few stairs until she could hand the plate to her benefactor. She smiled for the first time in days.. Milly took the plate and nodded.

"The neighbors, los vecinos," she said, gesturing towards the door across the landing. "Vuelven hoy, they will come back today."

"Esta bien, it's okay," said Fortuna. "Se fue la lluvia, no more rain."

Fortified by the unexpected breakfast, she packed up her belongings and left the stairwell. It was sunny and pleasant outside and she sat for a while on the bench by the street. Since it was Sunday, the thrift store would be closed.

She had been thinking of trading in *The Great Gatsby* for another book.

"I love the picture on the front," she told Ofelia, "but I don't care about East coast rich people. The man gazing at a light across the water, longing for something out of reach, that I understand. And that part at the very beginning, that the rich guy has a gift for hope. That's me, too. But most of the people in the story are of bad character, the women especially are spoiled and cruel."

As she was thinking about the strange story, a tall, dark woman in a light-colored dress and sandals walked up the street and turned onto the sidewalk to the art gallery. Fortuna recognized the girl from Old Town Road. She looked Indian, maybe from one of the Pueblos around Albuquerque. Like Fortuna herself, she was uncommonly tall and dark. She thought of the tennis playing socialite in the Gatsby book, except with dark skin. The woman tried the door to the gallery. When she found it locked, she took a key from the pocket of her dress, opened the door and went inside.

"I hope she's not involved with that malcriado who lives there. She is certainly too good for him. Maybe she is there for the boy."

When the girl didn't reemerge after an hour, Fortuna crossed the street with her suitcase and wended her way through the narrow streets of Old Town to the sculpture garden behind the museum. She took out her book to give it another try. Soon she had lost track of time, absorbed in the unimaginable parties, affairs and the terrible fate of Myrtle. Fortuna was repelled but also fascinated by the lives of these strange people. The sun was going down.

Fortuna was wary of returning to the bench that had seemed such a refuge a few nights earlier but she was also concerned about the young boy who seemed to be hiding in the gallery.

"He is so young, like Billy but Billy has family and this boy is alone," she said. "Maybe if I stay close, I might be able to help him, to let him know I can see that he is in trouble."

She crossed the parking lot and walked past the house where she first saw the boy and headed down the street towards the Alameda Drain, on the lookout for another refuge before darkness fell. When she reached the end of the block, it started to rain again. A house on the corner looked abandoned, the yard filled with trash and weeds, its stucco disintegrating and the windows boarded up. But it had a portal over the entryway and the rusty gate was standing open so she dragged her suitcase up the two steps until she no longer felt the raindrops.

She was sheltered from the rain but the wind had begun to blow and she was already wet. The screens on the outside door were in tatters and Fortuna thought the front door was ajar. She would ordinarily never enter such a house but the rain and the wind were making her teeth chatter. She pushed the door open and was hit with a terrible stench from inside, obviously others had already found this place. She saw a body splayed out in one corner. Homeless drug addicts.

She closed the door as quickly and quietly as possible, hoping none of the house's occupants had noticed her presence so she could stay on the porch under the portal. But she could hear someone stirring and muttering inside, so she dragged the suitcase out to the sidewalk and unstrapped the umbrella, just as a man with bushy hair in stained trousers appeared in the doorway.

"Hey lady, you want to come inside?" he leered at her. Fortuna kept walking, struggling with her one good hand to keep the umbrella over her while pulling the suitcase.

"You got any money?" he yelled after her. She walked faster.

Turning the corner by the acequia, she headed back towards Central, checking behind her to make sure the man had not followed her. The street was deserted. It began to rain harder and she tightened her grip on the umbrella, only to drop the handle of her suitcase. She would not get far juggling these two items with one hand. She felt a wave of hopelessness washing over her. Where could she go to stay dry until the rain stopped? She had been chased out of so many places, it was hard to know where to go next.

A few soggy steps later, she found herself at the foot of the empty lot where she had taken refuge from the sun on the day after the boy ran into the river. There were no lights anywhere along the long stretch of dirt and weeds but she could just make out the outline of the tree where she passed that hot afternoon that now seemed so long ago. With no other options she could see, she dragged herself, suitcase and umbrella, towards the tree, trying to avoid the mud puddles forming around her. She glanced up and noticed what looked like Christmas lights twinkling from an upstairs balcony and she was cheered in spite of everything. A gift for hope.

Gus

As soon as he got to work and clocked in, Gus called his uncle. "Oye tio, I had to move the kid," he said. "That guy Tony brought over a girl and they got drunk outside in the car. He passed out and she crashed the car into the wall of Rumaldo's house. The police came. They didn't see Leo but the gas company and the insurance appraiser will come today so I had to find another place for him."

"Que chinga," said Manuel. "Is he at the house with you?"

"No, Tony left to bail out his girlfriend and wanted to give me the drugs for Leo, but you know I can't have anything to do with that shit. This guy, Rod, who runs that gallery across the parking lot offered to let Leo stay in the bedroom in the back. He said he didn't mind giving him the drugs."

Manuel was quiet. Finally he said, "I understand mi hijito but what do we know about this Rod? I don't know what Leo's father will say about bringing a stranger into this mess."

"Well then he should come get his kid!" said Gus. "This is not our problem. The kid is sick and needs help but there's nothing I can do for him. Rod is being helpful but he wants to know when Leo will be leaving. It's a hassle for him too."

"Okay," said Manuel. "Let me talk to his old man and see what he wants to do. I thought he and the kid were in communication."

"I think Leo's phone battery is dead," said Gus. "My charger won't fit his phone."

"Then keep yours on today," said Manuel. "Mute it if you need to but don't turn it off in case I need to get in touch."

Gus put his phone on mute, stuck it in his back pocket so he would feel it vibrate if someone was calling and started frying up bacon and sausage for the breakfast crowd.

"Any news on the shooting on Friday?" he asked the other cooks.

"Customers still talking about it, but they never found the guy," said a waitress waiting for her order. "I think they finally took down the roadblock at the bridge but I'm not sure. Haven't been down that way."

Gus thought about calling Julia. Surely she had read about the killing in the newspaper or seen it on the TV news. But she might not realize that it happened outside his restaurant. He could make it sound like he just wanted to reassure her that he was okay. But he didn't want to tie up his phone until he heard back from Manuel.

A couple of hours later, Manuel called. Gus signaled to the other cooks that he was going on break and walked out the diner's back door to the alley where the dumpsters were overflowing. A pair of homeless people were going through the trash. Ordinarily, Gus would have shooed them away, but today he was preoccupied. He walked down the driveway where he could not see them and they could not hear his conversation.

"Tucker says leave him where he is for now," said Manuel. "He's talking to a judge in Santa Fe who's a friend. They're trying to negotiate a deal for Leo."

Gus was confused. He thought Leo was running from some drug-related hassle. Why would a judge be involved? The truth came over him in a flash: the kid was the shooter. He matched the description on the news. Suddenly it all made sense, why hadn't he put it together before? But now he was really worried about becoming involved. But he was already involved.

"Tucker wants the name and phone number of the guy at the gallery," Manuel said. "Tell him he will be paid for his trouble. But in the meantime, Tucker says don't give him a phone charger. Better that he doesn't have a way to call any of his friends."

"He's just a kid," Gus said. "He'll just be sent to juvie somewhere. How much more of a deal can he get?"

Manuel laughed. "He looks like a kid but he's older than you," he said. "He's small and has a baby face but he's got a long history of trouble behind him. I told Tucker he can't stay where he is much longer but he's still trying to figure something out. He says just another day or two at the most."

Gus hoped this was going to work for Rod. He hadn't taken a close look at those pills Leo was taking, but he hoped there were enough in that bottle to buy him another forty-eight hours. Gus had no experience with

Oxycontin but he knew what it was like to withdraw from heroin. It was hard to imagine that a bunch of pills could control that for long.

On his lunch break, he ran home. He needed to make sure things were quiet there before he could concentrate on his job. Three men were standing by the place where Desiree hit the wall with the car. One was an old man who he assumed was his uncle's friend Rumaldo. He was applying plaster to the damaged wall. The others were wearing uniforms. Gas company, he thought. He walked over and joined them.

"I'm Gustavo," he said. "I live there," he said, pointing to his uncle's house. "Manuel is my uncle."

The old man held out his hand. "Much gusto," he said. "I am Rumaldo. This is my house. Did you see what happened?"

"Si," replied Gus. "The girl and her boyfriend were staying at my house, just for the night. I guess she got upset and tried to leave in his car but she didn't get far."

"Que chinga," said Rumaldo. "You should find some new friends."

"They aren't my friends," Gus said. "My Tio Manuel asked me to let them stay for the night as a favor for his boss. I'm sorry for the damage to your house but I'm glad they're gone."

Rumaldo shook his head and went back to his task.

Gus went to the gallery door but Rod had put up the CALL FOR APPOINTMENT sign but there was no phone number. He knocked softly but no one answered. Maybe Rod's catching up on his sleep because of all the commotion last night. He headed back to the diner.

On his afternoon break, he decided to text Julia. He wanted to talk about the murder but he was reluctant to get into it with his co-workers since he knew much more than they did and might let something slip. He hoped she would see that he was upset and was contacting her for advice and would not see this as violating the terms of their understanding.

"It's crazy around here," he wrote. "There was a murder in front of the diner two days ago."

He hit send, put his phone in his pocket and went back into the kitchen, determined not to stress about whether she answered or not. In just a few minutes, his phone vibrated. He looked and there was a text from Julia. He held his breath and opened it.

"OMG I read about that!" she wrote. "Are you okay? Did you see it?"

"Only after," Gus wrote. "It was bad, lots of blood."

"You be careful down there!!!" Julia wrote.

Gus wondered if he could tell her that he might know who did it, even if he didn't say the kid was living at his house. It would be a secret between them and would show that he trusted her. But could he trust her? She was so straight, maybe she would tell her parents and they would call the police. He would have to think about it a bit more.

"I will," he texted her. "You be careful too."

He put his phone back in his pocket and went back to work. Later, on his way home, he stopped by the gallery again. The door was still locked. He knocked softly, no response. He tried peeking through the blinds on the French doors and could see Rod lying on what seemed to be a futon. He looked asleep. Gus couldn't think of anything else to do so he went home and watched a baseball game on TV. Occasionally he would step outside to see if any lights came on across the way, but they never did.

Leo

The smack he got from Rod lasted most of the day. Leo drifted in and out of sleep, snorting a bit more whenever he began waking up. When it was gone and he became restless, he got up from the bed and went out into the gallery. Rod was asleep on the futon behind the desk but he stirred when Leo came into the room.

It was still daylight and it seemed a strange time for a gallery to be locked up but his brain fog was too thick to figure out what might be happening. Maybe it was Sunday, he had lost track of time. If he thought he could break into that drawer of cash without waking Rod, he'd be doing it right now. But with no phone and no money, there was nowhere to go. He wished he hadn't left the gun in the bosque. It would be useful right now. If Rod woke up he could use it to scare him, at least. Give himself time to get out of town with some of that cash.

He went into the bathroom, raised the toilet seat and peed for a long time. Must be that coke he chugged. As he zipped up his jeans, he heard the gallery door open. He waited to see who would walk into his line of sight and was surprised to see a tall, dark-skinned woman. She did not see him, but was focused on Rod, still asleep on the futon. She crossed the room and sat down beside him, which seemed to finally wake him.

"Hey," Rod murmured. She seemed familiar.

"I'm Paloma, remember me?" she said. "I brought some supplies for your friend."

It was the girl from the house on Hollywood. She was beautiful, just like he remembered, but there was something different. She smiled winningly at Rod. The last time he saw her she looked defeated. Now she was...alluring. She sat on the edge of the futon and held out a canvas pouch. Rod sat up and looked inside: it was a set of works and a few baggies of white powder. His mouth tasted like sour milk and probably smelled like it too. He needed a few minutes to collect himself and clean up a bit before interacting with this hot goddess. He pointed to the bedroom. "He's in there." She started down the short hallway to where Leo stood, leaning against the doorframe.

Leo was coming down from the drugs but watching Paloma approach was still a heavenly vision. He was anxious to get his hands on the drugs she brought, but it occurred to him that he wouldn't mind getting my hands on her too. From her mahogany skin and long black hair to her long legs and not-too-small breasts he could see through her diaphanous blouse, she was a walking dream. She reminded him a bit of that girl he got into in rehab, sexy in a serious kind of way. What was her name? Oh yeah, Julia.

Julia had different addictions but he knew her inside and out. The night he found out that his best friend overdosed, Julia had tried to calm and comfort him. She had that maternal thing like many girls and Leo knew how to use it to his advantage. She sat with him on the stairs and stroked his arm, held his hand. Before long they were kissing and after that, he never loosened his emotional grip on her. He fucked her in the woods behind the hospital nearly every day during recreation periods. They didn't get undressed in case they had to reappear quickly and seem to be exercising. Actually they were exercising, he thought, and who cared about the clothes.

Leo had a way with women when he wanted to employ it and his success led him to be cocky about his appeal. But he knew he was incapable of giving Paloma a good fuck in his present state. Maybe he could get her number, reconnect when he was in better shape, especially if he managed to leave with some of the cash he had discovered. Rod seemed to be doing a lot of sleeping since he appropriated the bottle of Oxy. It might not be too hard to grab some of it on his way out. But first things first.

Leo sat on the edge of the bed to prepare his fix. But the girl had left the room. As he took his shot, he could hear her talking to Rod in the gallery.

"Is that your red Fiat parked over at the house?" she asked.

"Yeah, you like it?" Rod replied. In Paloma's absence he had brushed his teeth and slicked back his hair, trying to conceal the grey underneath what remained of the brown.

"I'll take you for a drive if I can get somebody to cover for me here," he said. "Any chance of that? Do any of the guys at the house ever come over here to work?"

"Nobody ever worked here until you came," she said. "What about the kid? Can he watch over it for a while?"

Leo couldn't let that pass. He walked a few steps into the room.

"I'm not a kid," he said with his most engaging grin. "It's just my youthful look. But I'm just passing through. I got a gallery in Santa Fe I need to get back to."

"Too bad," said Paloma, but she was looking at Rod. She was sitting very close to him on the edge of the futon. What did she see in that aging loser? Leo couldn't imagine those two together. She was way too good for his sorry ass. But whatever, later for her. Leo went back to the bedroom to enjoy his high in peace.

Paloma

Paloma's father was from Laguna Pueblo, but she barely knew him. He had sisters, so she had cousins there.. She was taken for summer visits when she was very young, but hadn't been there in many years. Raised by a single mother from Mexico who managed the Dairy Queen across the road from their Pojoaque apartment building, Paloma resembled her paternal grandmother, who was also tall and dark.

Paloma did well at school. She had friends and played volleyball, at which she excelled because of her height. She had a few casual boyfriends who took her on movie dates or to dinner in Espanola.

Her girlfriends were all losing their virginity halfway through high school, but Paloma resisted.

"It's not that I'm saving it for marriage," she told them, "I just need it to be special."

That plan died in her senior year when her prom date, egged on by his drunken friends, put something in her drink. When she woke up on the golf course with a pain between her legs and her half-dressed date passed out next to her, she knew that all her high-minded plans had been for nothing. Life does to you what it will. She never saw that boy again and didn't attend her high school graduation.

She started UNM in the fall, thanks to the state lottery scholarship program. She made a few friends, but was reluctant to join in social activities for fear of a repeat of the high school horror. Paloma would have loved to be a doctor but without encouragement and financial help, that seemed unlikely so she decided to study sports medicine. She did well in her classes and began to be invited to dinners and parties given by professors and teaching assistants, who seemed safer than college boys her age.

At a reception at the Hispanic Cultural Center, she was introduced by one of the organizers to Antonio. He was older, no doubt, but he was suave and charming, qualities Paloma rarely saw in men. He was tall—

taller than her—and deeply tanned. His hair had streaks of gray and he was dressed in a three-piece suit, much more formal than most of the other men there. She found him attractive -- like Antonio Banderas or Julio Iglesias. Handsome older men who were not real.

"What are you studying?" he asked, looking at her with what seemed like a paternal interest.

"Sports medicine," she said. "I wanted to be a pediatrician but my family couldn't afford the schooling. I'm at UNM on the lottery scholarship."

"Smart girl," he said with a smile. "As it happens, I am getting ready to open a sports wellness center here in Albuquerque. There might be a job for you there after you get your degree."

Her face told him she was interested.

"Give me your phone number and we can have lunch one day next week," he said. "I'll tell you more about it then."

She fished in her purse for a pen and wrote her number on the cocktail napkin under her glass of club soda. He put it in his breast pocket, bowed his head at her and went to join another group. She watched him make the rounds of the room and then leave without seeming to be aware of her. She wondered if he really would call her.

He did and she went to lunch with him several times to talk about his plans. One day, he announced that he had found a location and wanted her to see it. He drove her to a big adobe house on Old Town Road with an enormous yard surrounded by an iron fence and a locked gate. Paloma was confused. It didn't look like a good place for a sports wellness center.

"I forgot that the plans are still here in my office," he said. "You'll get a better idea of what the layout will be if you can see those too. As long as we're here, why don't you come see the house? It was built by a daughter of one of the founding families and there are two hundred-year-old bultos in the library."

By this time, Paloma trusted Antonio completely. He had never treated her with anything but a respectful, almost fatherly interest. So she was shocked to her core when he grabbed her as soon as they were inside the door. He pushed her up against the wall and tried to kiss her. When she turned her head away, he slapped her. She started to cry.

"Please no. I need to go. I need to go home."

"Not just yet, my girl," he said.

He assaulted her over a period of three days, unmoved by her tears and pleas.

"If you let me go home, I will never tell anyone. Please, they will be looking for me," she lied.

No one would notice she didn't return to the dorm. She had no close friends who would care. Paralyzed with fear and shame, Paloma never returned to school. She also began to take some of the drugs she was offered, just to dull the edges of his new reality but not so much that she was incapable of planning her escape. It was her constant preoccupation since the beginning. She had not seen her purse after the first day so she had no phone, no money and no identification but she was determined to get away somehow.

Antonio had a posse of young men who came and went from the house on Old Town Road but obviously lived elsewhere. After a few months, Antonio had to return to Mexico on business and he sent her to the house on Hollywood where Juan and the others could keep an eye on her. They were careful not to give her an opportunity to escape but she was unfailingly kind to them, treating them like her brothers, folding their laundry and supplying homecooked dinners. Eventually, they relaxed their surveillance and allowed her to have a garden in the back of the house. She was also used as a short-run courier to the gallery, whose proximity to the house made escape unlikely. She would definitely need help.

G

Gus

Gus woke before dawn, thinking about Julia. He felt most horny at this time of day. His uncle used to play a Ferlin Husky song called "Four in the Morning "and he always thought about it at these times.

"It's four in the morning and once more the dawning/has woke up the wanting in me." He sang the song in his head and wondered what it would be like to wake up next to Julia. He felt a physical longing that was undeniable.. Maybe if he confided in her about Leo, it would bring them closer together. They would have a secret. He decided that he would take this chance and trust her. He couldn't go back to sleep but lay awake anxiously awaiting an acceptable time to contact her. He decided to do it right before leaving for work.

"Hey. I had a rough night, trying to figure out what to do about something. Maybe you can help me."

He didn't have to wait long for a reply. Good, he probably didn't wake her up.

"I'm here, what's going on?"

"Remember the murder I saw at the restaurant? The killer is here, staying across the driveway."

"Oh my God, how do you know that?"

"He's the son of my uncle's boss. He's all strung out."

A few minutes passed before she replied.

"Who's your uncle's boss? You mean that rich gallery owner in Santa Fe?"

"Yes. The son's name is Leo and he's a real mess. His father is trying to fix it up I guess."

"Why is he staying across the parking lot?"

"I wouldn't let him stay here because he's on drugs and I'm staying far away from that (for reasons you know lol). The guy across the way has a gallery with a room in back and offered to let him stay until his father collects him."

"Wow, that's quite a story! Are you still on Rio Grande, across from the Plaza?"

"Yes. Listen Julia, please keep this to yourself. Don't call the cops or anything like that. If the kid gets popped, it will be bad for my uncle."

"Okay I promise. But what kid are you talking about?"

"The kid...Leo."

"How old is he?"

"I don't know, looks young. I have to go to work TTYL"

Gus grabbed his keys and headed for the gallery to check on Rod and Leo. That went well, he thought. She seemed interested in what was going on and did promise not to tell. So maybe it would be something to keep him in her thoughts while they were apart. He worried that she would forget him and find someone else before he could fulfill his promise of one year's sobriety.

He knocked lightly on the door to the gallery. After a few minutes he knocked again and heard someone stirring inside. Rod, in his underwear, opened the door a crack. His graying hair was sticking up in the back.

"Everything okay with the kid?" Gus asked.

"Yeah, he's fine, still sleeping," Rod growled.

"Okay, just checking in before work," Gus said, backing away. "Didn't get an answer when I came by last night."

"I haven't been feeling well so I went to bed early," said Rod. "Still not feeling great, you might not want to get too close."

"Well, feel better and I guess I'll catch you later," Gus said. "Tell Leo his father is arranging things and will be in touch soon."

Rod closed the door and Gus headed for the diner.

He came home on his lunch break to find an unfamiliar car parked in front of the house. Gus peered inside, trying to guess whose car it might be, when a familiar voice startled him.

"Hey Gus, longtime no see."

Julia came around the corner of Rumaldo's building with a sack of burritos from Sofia's on the corner.

She looked even more beautiful than the last time he saw her, getting into her father's car to leave the rehab hospital. She had gotten healthy there, so she already looked pretty good. But now, she was just flat-out gorgeous, he thought. Her curly blond hair was tied back and fell down her back and her eyes sparkled. In the hospital she had been pale and watery-eyed and spent little time on her appearance. When she came close to give him a hug, she smelled like something good to eat, and he said so.

Julia laughed. "It's the burritos, I got two just in case you came back before I ate them both."

"I'm so surprised," Gus said. "Good surprised but I never expected to see you here."

"Can we go inside and eat these?" She brandished the bag of burritos. "I will explain."

Gus unlocked the door and gestured her inside. He was so pleased with himself for daring to tell her his secrets. Look at how well it had turned out!

"What are you doing here?" he asked as she unwrapped the burritos. "Were you worried about me being involved with a criminal? It's okay, really. I don't even see him anymore."

Julia busied herself with napkins and didn't look at him.

"No, I trust your judgment to take care of yourself," she said. "But I thought I might be able to help. I know Leo."

Gus was stunned, disappointed and fearful all at the same time.

"How is that?"

"I know him from the Cottonwood Rehab up at Eagle's Nest," she said. "It was my first time and he helped me. I thought maybe I could help you both, maybe take him home and off your hands."

Gus let that sink in, trying to wrap his head around her and Leo. He knew she had been in a hospital for drugs before their stay at Another Chance.

"He's staying over there at the gallery across the parking lot," he said. "But I went over this morning before work and he was asleep or passed out. The guy who runs the gallery is sick so he closed it up. He thinks he may be infectious and told me not to come in. Leo's strung out but he has Oxys to get him through it."

"But can't we just get Leo out of there somehow? She asked. "As long as he has drugs, I could get him home."

"His father doesn't want him home yet," Gus said. "He's trying to work a deal for Leo through his political friends."

"But is he okay?" She seemed concerned, very concerned.

"I haven't seen him today but I think he's okay," Gus said. "I'm sure Rod would have contacted me if there was a problem."

"Is that the gallery owner? Rod?"

"Yeah, he seems okay. He offered to help since it would be hard for me."

Gus gave her what he hoped was a significant look. Did she remember what he had promised her, and why? He was too confused to know, but his lunch break was over.

"I have to get back to work," he said. "Can you wait here for me? I'll be off at five. You can watch TV, take a nap, whatever. Just make yourself at home."

"Okay, sure," she said. She didn't seem to mind that he was leaving. "I'll see you later."

Reluctantly, Gus went back to work. He spent the afternoon flipping burgers and checking the time, which seemed to have slowed to a glacial pace. He couldn't work out why Julia had come. She had refused to see him until he stayed clean for a year, yet here she was, going the extra sixty miles between Santa Fe and Albuquerque to try to help a stone addict with apparently no plans to get clean. What was she thinking?

He went back over all the episodes of their friendship. He had noticed her right away at the hospital and had gravitated to her kindness and beauty. But she had been one of the patients who went down to the basement twice a week for electroshock therapy, and when she came back to the dayroom she would introduce herself to him and to the others in the dayroom. Gus had been in the hospital long enough to know that memory loss was a given. It scared him enough to refuse the treatment for himself, even though the patients who took it did seem more peaceful and happier for days afterwards. He envied them that, but the memory loss part scared him. What if he could never remember anything? He might end up like some of the older residents who just paced and muttered to themselves.

After a few weeks, Julia stopped getting ECT and their relationship became more predictable. They ate meals together and took walks around the grounds. Once he worked up the courage to hold her hand and she allowed it, but she would not let him kiss her. He was disappointed, but thought it demonstrated her modesty and high self-esteem and that she was unwilling to lead him on when they were both at such a difficult place in their lives. Was that the kind of friendship she had with Leo too? Would she have dropped everything and come to him if he was in trouble? He wouldn't have expected it.

On a break, he sent her a text. "Okay? I will be home a few minutes after five and we can go check on Leo." He kept checking his phone but got no response. The last two hours of his shift seemed to drag on for days. When five o'clock arrived, he hung up his apron, clocked out, then ran all the way home.

Julia

She was a smart girl, daughter of two materials scientists who worked at Los Alamos National Laboratory. She had grown up on The Hill and attended Los Alamos High. The school sent more graduates to college, particularly Ivy League colleges, than any other school in the state, but Julia was not among them. She did well in school, but instinctively rebelled against her parents' high expectations and strict rules. She started sneaking out of the house at night to join her friends at Ashley Pond, first to smoke pot and eventually sample pills taken from her friends' parents' medicine cabinets. Oxycontin was Julia's particular favorite. It gave her a happy, dreamy feeling that made sex with various guys—some of them older failure-to-launch types still hanging around—comfortable enough, if not at all thrilling. At school, she was always partial to the stoners and fuck-ups, despite her own academic prowess.

Julia's parents were frustrated that their only daughter showed little interest in post-secondary schooling and they eventually acquiesced to Julia's request for a gap year, even though she had no firm plans about how she would spend it. That became a moot point after the car accident. She began her gap year working as a receptionist at the Lab's Biology Department by day and partying every night at the White Rock Overlook with the town underachievers. One winter night driving back from one such party she misjudged a curve and ran her car off the road and luckily, into a tree. If the tree had not intervened, she and her Audi would have been at the bottom of the canyon. In the end, only her leg was broken. The injury clipped her wings somewhat since she could not drive, but she discovered Oxycontin, which took the edge off her confinement. After a few weeks, the pain had diminished but she told the doctor she couldn't sleep because of the discomfort and he kept refilling the prescription. Since she didn't need the drugs for pain, they became recreational for her and her pals at the Overlook. But eventually, the doctor failed to approve the scrip renewal, offering to refer her to a therapist to deal with her sleep issues. The day after her pills ran out, Julia encountered withdrawal for the first time. Every bone in her body ached, she had nausea, chills and a terrible headache. She called in sick to her job and after her parents went to work, she called Kevin, one of the older guys who hung out at the Overlook and with whom she had shared her drugs and her body from time to time.

"Dude, I am so sick," she croaked. "The doc cut me off my meds."

"That's harsh," he said. "I can get some good quality heroin from my buddy down in the Valley. It's the only thing that works on Oxy withdrawal."

"Oh man, I don't know," Julia said. "That's major. And I hate needles. I can't do that."

"No worries," Kevin said. "You can just snort it, it still works. It's really no different than coke, just has the opposite effect. You can just use it until your Oxy withdrawal symptoms go away. Just don't do too much and don't increase what you use when you start getting used to it."

Julia was so miserable she was willing to try something drastic so she agreed. But she was enough of a hedonist that she came to love the heroin high. Not only did she not resist the temptation to increase her use, one night she allowed Kevin to inject it into her arm and that was it. She was a for real junkie.

It took a while for her parents to catch on, but eventually they found her stash in her purse when they could not wake her up for work one morning. They sent her to rehab far away from her gang in Los Alamos, but there she met Leo. She first saw him at a group therapy meeting. He came in late, accompanied by a staff member, after he declined to attend voluntarily. Julia had considered trying to avoid communing with her fellow inmates but she was too tired from the methadone they gave her to fight about it. She recognized Leo as a fellow rebel, but he was also really cute, she thought. He was blond and boyish but up close the years of substance abuse had started to show. Julia chalked it up to hard living and looked for an opportunity to connect with him outside of group. Her chance came the next night when Leo received a phone call informing him that his best friend and running buddy had died of an overdose. Leo became unwound by the news. Julia dissuaded the nurse who was preparing a syringe to medicate his despair and said she would try to calm him. She found him outside sitting in the tall grass before the woods. She sat down beside him and he allowed her to hug him tightly as he trembled and wept. She whispered in his ear that it would be alright, that she would take care of him. Eventually, he stopped shaking and they walked back to the hospital hand in hand. After that night, they were inseparable. When Julia's parents announced their intention to seek her release to home confinement after six weeks, she resisted.

"I'm not sure I'm ready to face being home," she said, unwilling to face her life without Leo. "Everyone at home is on drugs."

"Oh come on Julia, that's not so," her mother said.

"Well, everyone I know, anyway."

This bought her another week, but psychiatric beds were in short supply, so finally her parents came back and loaded Julia and her belongings in the SUV. Leo did not see her off. He was in his room playing with a GameBoy when Julia came to say she was leaving. He beckoned to her to come closer so he could give her a swift kiss.

"I'll look you up when I get out," he said. "It's been fun."

Julia didn't know how to take this tepid goodbye. She was smart enough to know what it meant but her brain tried frantically to find another explanation for his indifference. Maybe he didn't want her to see how much he would miss her. Since the meltdown when his friend died, he hadn't been particularly forthcoming about his feelings. She tried to keep in touch after her release, writing long letters that were never answered. Maybe he just wasn't the letter-writing type, she told herself. Her parents got her another clerical job at the Lab and tried unsuccessfully to interest her in applying to college for the fall semester. The combination of parental pressure and Leo's silence led her back to her old gang and her old habits. Because of her hospitalization, she had to be piss tested at work but she managed to have her tests scheduled in advance, rather than randomly, and one of her friend's younger sister made a cottage industry of providing clean piss to Los Alamos employees. But although she had promised herself she would not go back to heroin, within a month she had rationalized a taste, and then another. Eventually she was addicted again.

She had told her parents that she had a second job at the record store in town, which sponsored weekly concerts in the store parking lot, so she would have an excuse to be out every night. But eventually they discovered the ruse and began watching her, searching her room when she was out and trailing her as inconspicuously as possible. She started to miss work and word of that got back to her father. He also knew when she was fired, although she tried to keep it a secret. She was soon back on her way to rehab, this time in a more remote facility that would treat her addiction and the depression she fell into after being ghosted by Leo. She had tried to run away when she learned that her parents were going to recommit her and she fought with the town cops who found her and brought her home. So her parents decided to let the doctors try shock therapy.

She was scared the first time she went down the stairs to the room in the hospital basement used for electroshock therapy, known as ECT. No one had said that it was painful, but that wasn't comforting since they couldn't remember anything about the past twenty-four hours. But although the memory loss was disorienting at first, she came to like the feeling. It gave her permission to believe in her imagination and to lie. There was a guy at the hospital—Gus—who was obviously taken with her and she appreciated his attention and admiration, although he was definitely not her type. He was earnest about getting sober and making a better life for himself, wanted a family and the sort of suburban life that Julia was fleeing. But her memory issues allowed her to gloss over the events that led to her being confined at the hospital and receiving shock therapy. She came clean about her heroin use after being cut off opioids, but attributed her depression to a difficult relationship with her parents, who she accused of neglecting her while participating in key parties with the town swingers. Julia knew a little about those parties because her friend Kevin's parents were part of that crowd and regaled her with stories about what he had seen when his parents thought he was asleep. Julia's parents would have been horrified to have anyone think they condoned, much less participated, in such a party. But Gus hung on her every word and obviously believed them all. She recognized that he had not known many girls like her and was fascinated for that reason, but he was also a genuinely nice guy who very much wanted to know her and help her. The last thing she wanted. But it was useful to have him with her while she was at the hospital, although she stopped him once when he tried to kiss her. She told him that she was wary of involvement with former addicts until she knew that she had her own sobriety well in hand. They agreed to wait a year after both went home to get back together, just to make sure they had not relapsed. But although she appreciated the unconditional positive regard she got from Gus, she never thought of him unless he contacted her. When he did, she would reply politely, but was careful not to be too encouraging. But at the same time, she was obsessively looking for Leo. The hospital wouldn't say whether he had been released so she wrote him letters there that went unanswered. She drove down to Santa Fe and visited his father's gallery, hoping she might run into him there. When that didn't happen, she tried to chat up the staff. Had Leo been there lately? (No) Did they have any idea where he was living? (Who knows?) She asked to see Tucker but he was not at the gallery that day. She left a message for him to call her but he didn't. Every morning she would google Leo's name hoping for some clue about where he was. So when she heard that Leo was with Gus and in trouble, she told her boss she was sick, gassed up her car and headed south.

R

Rod

When he awoke from his drug-induced sleep, Rod believed the girl might have been a dream. She was so beautiful and seemed to have some interest in him. He had been used to that when he was younger, but as his life started its downhill slide his charm became less reliable. He couldn't remember the last time a really attractive woman had come on to him. He had some success with the girls at the casino, but they didn't have the class of this Paloma. He still thought highly enough of himself that he was willing to believe that she found him interesting, but something told him to be cautious.

When he first saw her at the house on Hollywood, she was with the big man who seemed to be the boss. She did not look happy and might be looking for a way out, but helping her would not help his standing with this organization and might be downright dangerous. Still, he had thrilled to the touch of her hands when she awakened him...soft and gentle. He could go for some more of that. But he might have to stop taking the Oxys, as much as he loved the feeling. He would never be able to fuck her if he kept that up. Can't get it up if you keep it up.

His reveries were interrupted by a knock at the door. Probably Gus again, he thought, hauling himself up from the futon, but maybe the lovely Paloma again. He opened the door to find not Gus or Paloma, but a pretty young Anglo girl. Baby spinner, he thought involuntarily. She was just the right size.

"Hi, are you Rod?" she said. "I'm Julia. I'm a friend of Gus and Leo. Is he awake?" She did not smile or seem particularly interested in who he was, looking past him, actually. She was obviously on a mission and he didn't have the energy to interfere with it.

"Back there," he said, indicating the door to the bedroom. "Whether he's awake, your guess is as good as mine."

She brushed past him and crossed through the gallery, without a glance at any of the art or his futon with its mess of sheets and pillows. She opened the door to the bedroom.

"Leo," she said softly. Her voice had a whole different tone, one that Rod recognized instantly. In his younger days he'd had his share of girls looking to seduce him.. But listening to that silky tone got him going.

She seemed to become aware of his presence behind her and kicked the door closed with one of her high-heeled boots. It only closed halfway. Rod retreated to his desk across the room but had a slice of a view into the bedroom while he scrolled through his phone messages. Leo had not moved when she called his name and she was now sitting on the bed, stroking his back, which was turned to her.

"Leo, it's Julia," she purred. He didn't move. She leaned closer, resting her head on his shoulder and whispering to him. Rod couldn't make out what she was saying but he recognized the insinuation in it. She draped her arm over him and appear to be rubbing his stomach, but maybe not exactly. Leo stirred and mumbled something about sleeping. When she persisted, he lifted his head and looked at her.

"What are you doing here?" he asked with more irritation than interest.

"I heard what happened," she said. "I wanted to help."

He dropped his head back on the pillow. Rod could barely hear him answer her.

"Unless you have drugs and money and a car, you can't help me," he said. "I really just need to sleep now."

"I have a car," she said. "When you're rested, I can drive you home."

Leo didn't answer.

"Shall I stay?" she asked. Again, no response. After a few minutes, she unzipped her boots and curled up behind him on the bed, once again draping her hand over him.

She knows what she's doing, Rod thought. She was young but hardly inexperienced. He knew that Leo was in no condition to respond to her overtures, but hell, neither was he. He was feeling headachy and low-energy. Another Oxy or two would fix that, but he was becoming pretty dysfunctional. He had not been asked to "sell" any paintings since Leo arrived. Since Juan knew the situation and was helping to keep him quiet, maybe things would go on like this for a while longer.

He crossed the room to the kitchenette. He took out his pills and found a sharp knife. Maybe half an Oxy would take care of the headache but he would still be able to keep his wits about him. He washed it down with what was left in a can of beer on the counter and went back to the futon to wait for the effects to take hold. Despite his efforts to stay awake, he soon dozed off again. When he awoke several hours later, someone was knocking on the door. There was no sound from the bedroom. He opened the door to find Paloma, looking beautiful as ever and somewhat taken aback by his disheveled appearance. His pants were kind of sagging and there was beer on his t-shirt.

He attempted to produce his most charming smile.

"Hey, you're back!"

She was less friendly than before.

"I brought some more stuff for the kid," she said. "Is he asleep?"

Without waiting for an answer, she brushed past him. He watched her standing in the doorway, looking at the scene with disapproval.

"Who is this girl?" she asked with her back to him.

"A friend of Leo's," he said. "She just showed up. I don't know how she knew he was here."

Julia disentangled herself from Leo and stood up, straightening her clothes.

"I have a car and I'd like to take him home to Santa Fe," she said.

At that, Leo suddenly came alive. He sat up.

"I'm not going with you to Santa Fe," he said. He did not look at her, but had his gaze fixed on Paloma. He had been dreaming of her in his twilight state ever since she first entered his room. He welcomed the drugs of course but he was envisioning a future with this gorgeous creature. But first he would have to get rid of Julia, who was seriously getting on his nerves.

"Look, Julia," he said, "it's nice of you to want to help and all, but I don't need a ride and I'm not going to Santa Fe. And you shouldn't be here, it could be dangerous for you."

He was saying the right things, but he still would not look at her. He continued staring at Paloma, wondering if she might be his way out.

"I don't care," Julia insisted. "I want to help."

Alright, he thought. No more Mr. Nice Guy.

"Julia, I need you to fuck off," he said. "I'm not going back and you're not coming with me. I'm sorry you came all the way down here for nothing but I didn't ask you to come."

Her eyes filled with tears but she tried to tough her way through. She picked up her purse and squeezed past her rival without a word. Rod unlocked the door. A minute after it closed, there was the sound of a car pulling out of the driveway.

Rod was not sorry to see her go, but he was none too pleased with the burgeoning friendship between Leo and Paloma. He would have been more alarmed to hear their whispered conversation as soon as he left the room. She was sitting next to Leo on the bed as he prepared his shot.

"I have money and I have a car," he lied. "They want me to deal drugs for them but I just want to get out of here. Will you help me?"

He figured he could take money from that drawer while Rod slept. By the time he awoke Leo would be long gone in his car. He didn't know exactly where it was parked, but he knew where to find the keys. How hard could it be to find the car?

Paloma did not answer but she gave him a long look as Rod came back into the room. She stood up, nodded to Leo and turned to go. Rod followed behind.

"I haven't eaten yet," he said. "Want to stay for some takeout?"

"No," she said without turning around. She slipped through the door and headed down the breezeway.

I guess that's that, Rod thought. Maybe he had gotten his signals crossed. Or maybe he should have taken a shower and changed clothes today. Whatever, who needs the bitch. After checking that Leo was dozing again in the bedroom, Rod took out his bottle of pills and took one, followed by the half he had left earlier. He washed them down with tap water in a plastic cup and went back to the futon to sleep. He would not wake up.

Fortuna

The tree was better than no shelter at all, but when the rain intensified, she was getting undeniably wet. There was no vegetation of any kind on the vacant lot, except for the occasional weed, so the ground became muddy very quickly. Fortuna found that if she stood up, she could press herself more closely to the wall that the tree overhung. On the other side of the wall was a large house with a large parking lot holding cars of all sorts, some shiny and new, some older and beat-up. There was also a large dog that she heard barking at passers-by on the street side, but he didn't seem to have noticed her nearness or picked up her scent.

Standing there with mud puddles growing near her feet, she looked up at the colorful flashing lights on the balcony that had so cheered her when she arrived. As she looked, a woman came out onto the balcony and stood watching the rain. Fortuna recognized Milly, her benefactor from earlier in the day. At the same time, Milly seemed to see her too. She gazed in her direction for a long minute, as if ascertaining if her eyes were seeing right. But Fortuna's height and carriage left little doubt. Milly began to gesture, seeming to beckon to her. Then she called in a loud, firm voice.

"Come inside!"

Fortuna was so grateful to be allowed back in the stairwell that she disregarded the mud that was now covering the soles of her shoes and the wheels of her suitcase. She managed to hold the umbrella and pull the suitcase with her one hand and slowly made her way back to the front of the building. When she arrived at the stairwell, Milly stood at the top of the stairs.

"Come inside," she said again, indicating her front door. "I made you a bed on the balcony. It won't be the Ritz but you will be dry."

Fortuna left her muddy shoes on the landing and picked up the suitcase by the handle. She was just barely able to carry it across the apartment and out the door to the brightly lit balcony, where Milly had moved all the furniture to one end and assembled some cushions and bedding in the other,

What was the Ritz, Fortuna wondered, but she felt a warmth move through her chest at this kind and totally unexpected offer. It was one thing to sleep in a stairwell protected from the rain, but being able to sleep flat with a pillow and blanket was a miracle. She hesitated, then decided she would still have to ask one more favor.

"Can I use the bathroom?" She dropped her eyes.

"Of course," said Milly. "I'll bring you a washcloth and I always have an extra toothbrush in case some boyfriend might want to stay over." Fortuna thought at her age she must be joking, but she had little experience with old Anglo ladies so she couldn't be sure.

She gratefully accepted the washcloth and toothbrush and got as much relieving and cleaning as she could out of the unexpected opportunity. When she emerged, the woman was standing in the bedroom doorway with a cotton nightgown and a bottle of water.

"You can wear this and hang your wet things over the balcony rail," she said. "When the rain stops, they will dry quickly."

She escorted Fortuna back to the balcony.

"Can I get you anything else before I go to bed?"

"No, thank you."

"I'm going to lock the balcony door," Milly said. "I hope you understand, I don't distrust you but I don't know you,"

"Claro," said Fortuna. "I will feel safe too."

Fortuna took off her wet dress and stockings and put on the cotton gown. As she settled down in her cushions and blankets, the colorful lights went out. Shortly thereafter, so did the bedroom light inside. It was the best night's sleep she had since leaving home.

She woke with the morning light, rose pink behind the houses to the west. She stood up, wrapping a light blanket around her against the chill and gazed at the new perspective she gained from the balcony. The tree in the lot next door looked far more insubstantial from above, no wonder it had not provided much protection from the rain. She also had a direct view of the big house with the cars and the dog. There was a man in the parking area pacing back and forth while talking on a cell phone. He seemed to be upset about something, but Fortuna was too far away to hear his conversation. Another man came out on the patio and called to him, but the pacing man turned his back and continued his phone call. The other man went back into the house.

"I wonder what is going on over there," she said to Ofelia. "There are too many cars for one family."

As Fortuna watched, a shiny black car with opaque tinted windows pulled into the driveway and waited for the gate to open, then drove into the parking area. A tall, stocky man in a black suit and sunglasses emerged from the back seat and went into the house. A few minutes later, he came out, followed by the young woman Fortuna had seen on the Plaza and again downstairs entering the gallery. She wore a simple shift dress and sandals, her hair coming loose from its braid. Even from a distance, Fortuna could tell she was unhappy, her pretty face expressionless and her proud carriage had slumped down to a defeated stance. As the man got back into the car, she opened the other door and sat with one leg still out of the car. Whatever was said between them, the woman was suddenly ejected from the car, falling hard on the concrete pavement with her leg twisted underneath her. Fortuna could hear her cry out in pain and the car door was slammed shut from inside and the car drove out of the gate. Fortuna felt her anger rising. She had come to feel protective of this tall, dark girl who did not exactly remind her of her daughter, but allowed her the fantasy of a perfect one. Like her, but better, more deserving of good fortune.

"Who could treat that lovely girl like that? That man doesn't deserve her. Why does she stay there?"

She thought of Myrtle in *The Great Gatsby* being run down on the road by the wealthy people who had used and discarded her. Was something like that going on at that house? She watched as the man who had been on the phone earlier came out of the house and helped the girl up from where she had been weeping on the ground. She took a step and cried out again. The man held her arm and led her limping into the house.

Fortuna was still shaking with fury when Milly, leaning on a cane, opened the door to the balcony and said "Buenas dias." She made a split second decision not to mention what she had seen. Perhaps if Milly thought she was gossiping and spying on the neighbors, she would no longer feel so compassionate.

"Would you like some coffee?"

Fortuna nodded. "Claro que si."

Milly disappeared into the kitchen, considering her situation. The afternoon rains would continue for several days and she would find it hard to turn Fortuna out in such weather. She had a soft heart but it had betrayed her more than once. Her instinct to rescue struggling people had sometimes been squandered on the usual sad collections of users and takers. But she had a feeling about Fortuna since the first day she observed her reading on the bench by the road. She was herself a voracious reader and felt a kinship with others who still read books.

Aside from sheltering in the stairway, Fortuna had taken no liberties and asked for no favors. She was quiet and uncomplaining.. Milly carried the steaming mug of coffee to Fortuna, then used her cane to drag a chair from the other end of the balcony. Fortuna sat back on her makeshift bed and sipped the coffee.

"Muchas gracias, esta bien."

"Me llama Milly," she said, and waited for her guest to reciprocate.

Fortuna hesitated, wondering if she could risk the truth with this person. But she was isolated and infirm and unlikely to know anyone who would be interested in her whereabouts.

"Me llama Fortuna," she said finally, relieved to be able to reveal herself to someone.

Milly decided to take a chance and press further.

"De donde vienes?"

"El norte," said Fortuna.

"What happened to your arm?"

"I fell down. It was an accident," Fortuna had gotten used to this lie so it came easily.

"Do you have no place to stay?"

"I am saving to fix my teeth," Fortuna said. Both women ignored the fact that she didn't answer the question. It was clearly all the information she would divulge. They sat in silence for a while, Milly pondering her options and Fortuna awaiting the verdict. Finally Milly spoke.

"The rains will come every day, the monsoons," she said. "You can stay here when they come and you can leave your things here if you want to go out when it's not raining, It broke my heart to see you trying to stay dry under that tree." She gestured to the muddy bog where Fortuna had sought shelter, the puddles drying up now in the morning sun.

"Gracias," Fortuna said, She felt a bit uneasy about leaving her suitcase with its dangerous contents in the care of this stranger, but Milly seemed honest and parking the suitcase would allow her to move about more quickly and would make her less conspicuous. She needed to visit the post office and find a pay phone to call her daughter-in-law.

"I accept your offer," she said. "Muy amable. But can I ask to use your bathroom again?"

"Claro que si," said Milly.

Fortuna pulled a brown dress from her suitcase and went into the bathroom to change and arrange her hair. She decided to leave off her hat, hopefully making her less recognizable. She took her dwindling funds from an envelope inside the suitcase and put them in the pocket of her dress.

"Me voy, I'll go now," she said, and carefully made her way down the stairs and towards the street.

Fortuna walked to the corner, where she ordered a burrito from Sofia's and sat in the walled back patio to eat it. It was liberating to be without the suitcase, which had been her constant companion since she arrived in Albuquerque. She had never felt safe leaving it anywhere before. From her table in the patio, she could see the balcony where she spent the night. She watched Milly come out and fold up the blankets and stack the cushions in a corner, but she didn't go near the suitcase. After that, Fortuna didn't worry about it again.

As she left the restaurant on her way to the post office on Central Avenue, she saw the dark girl crossing the street towards the Plaza. She was limping and had a bandage wrapped around her ankle. Where was she going? Fortuna could cut through the Plaza on her way to the post office so she followed her. The girl's injury slowed her down a bit so she was able to keep her in sight while she passed the stores on the south side of the Plaza and crossed the street onto Old Town Road, where Fortuna had first seen her. Instantly, she had that song in her head again.

Gonna take my horse to the Old Town Road/Gonna ride till I can't no more

Fortuna found herself nervously humming it as she followed the girl.

"I don't know why that song gets in my head and won't leave. It's like a spell."

The road skirted Tiguex Park, the other side of the street lined with new two-story adobe houses with spacious yards and locked gates. The girl stopped at one and rang the bell at the gate. She conversed with someone on an intercom who buzzed her in. The black car Fortuna had seen at the Hollywood house was parked in the driveway. The girl went inside and Fortuna sat on the grass at the park across the street and waited.

She thought she heard shouting and the sound of blows coming from the house but as she went to cross the street to hear better, it stopped. She waited a while longer but there was only silence.

"I wish there was something I could do for that girl, Ofelia, She has value but these men treat her like a dog. Less, they take pretty good care of their dogs."

A woman walking her dog stared at Fortuna as she passed. With her usual goal of not attracting attention, Fortuna reluctantly decided to end the surveillance and cut through the neighborhood streets to the post office, where her disability check would be waiting. She would cash it at the money store and find a phone to call up north. She needed to know that her Billy was safe. But the phone call was not reassuring.

"Billy is acting out again," her daughter-in-law Olivia said. "He seemed to be on the right track, doing some construction work and he applied to the community college to study computers. But he's back with the old crowd and going out every night until late. The construction work ended because he is unreliable."

Fortuna felt an actual pain in her heart. Billy was her vision of eternity, the grandson who would make her proud of having sacrificed for his sake.

"Have you been able to talk to him about what's going on? What caused him to change?"

"He won't talk. When I try, he says can't nobody tell him nothing. Where did he get such an idea?"

A memory stirred in Fortuna's head. That song she had been hearing all week about Old Town Road. It had that exact refrain: "Can't nobody tell me nothing."

On her way back to Milly's house, she stopped at the church on the Plaza. She didn't think she believed in God, not really. But old habits die hard and she kneeled to ask God or Jesus or whoever might be listening to save her grandson from the fate of so many young men up north. But all she could say was "Please, please, please help."

Gus

All afternoon Gus had been texting Julia with no response. On his break, he went outside and tried to call. No answer but he left a message.

"Where are you? I'm worried that you're not answering my texts. Please let me know you're okay. I'll be home at five."

Still, the afternoon passed with no word from her. When his shift was finally over, he clocked out and ran all the way home. Her car was gone. The door to the house was unlocked but she wasn't there. There was no note and no sign that she had spent any time there after he went to work. Gus crossed the parking lot to the gallery. The sign still said By Appointment Only and the door was locked. Peering through the blinds, Gus could see Rod on the futon, but when he knocked, Rod didn't move. He knocked louder, finally pounding on the door with the side of his hand. Finally, Leo came out of the bedroom and opened the door a few inches. He looked strung out but not in great distress.

"Sorry man, I guess Rod is taking a nap," Leo said. "I gave him one of my Oxys, he was having a bad day."

"Did you see Julia?" Gus asked. "She said you were friends and she wanted to help. I told her to wait until I got home before coming over."

"Yeah, she came over," Leo said, yawning. "She's just a chick from rehab, not sure how she found me but she shouldn't have bothered. I don't need all that drama in my life."

"What drama?" Gus didn't like the sound of that.

"We fucked some at the rehab, but she wanted it to be some big romance," Leo said. "Not gonna happen."

"So what, you sent her away?"

"Not exactly," Leo said. "She just left. Hey, when is my father going to come spring me from this dump?"

Gus was stunned, still digesting what he had just learned about Julia.

"I don't know," he said and went back to his house. All this time he had been organizing his life around her, trying to stay clean and avoid bad company, and she was chasing after some hardcore druggie with no intention of quitting. Who was she? How did he not pick up on how she was playing him? He would be ruminating on this for a very long time. He was grateful not to have any alcohol in the house or he would probably drink it. He considered going out to buy some, but that little voice in his head kept saying that maybe Leo was lying, maybe she had just offered a ride and he had refused. But why did she leave? And why did she not text him or leave a note?

After a few hours of contemplating all the different scenarios that might make this situation better than it seemed, he decided he needed to ask Leo some more questions about her visit. He crossed the parking lot and knocked on the door again. After getting no answer, he knocked again, louder. He turned the doorknob and the door opened. He stepped inside and called for Leo. No answer. He looked in the bedroom and it was empty. There was no one in the bathroom. It looked like Leo had just taken off. His father would not be pleased.

Gus went to Rod, asleep on the futon, and lightly shook his shoulder. It did not rouse him and Gus began to have a bad feeling about his unresponsiveness. He turned him onto his back and it was clear that Rod was dead. His face was swollen and turning blue on the side he had been laying on.

Gus jumped away, trying to take in what had happened. The bottle of Oxys was on Rod's desk. Who knows what was in those pills? There had been stories circulating about street pills being laced with Fentanyl, but Gus hadn't paid much attention since he was out of that world. Who knew where Tony had scored those pills.

But if Leo had gone, why didn't he take the drugs? He had been so fucked up a couple of hours earlier, he must still be taking them. But first, Gus needed to get out of the gallery and back to his house to decide what to do next. He would have to call his uncle to tell Leo's dad that he was gone. But first, he would need to wipe his fingerprints off the gallery door handle. He was not going to be connected to a drug overdose. And it was time to find another place to live. Immediately.

He looked around to see if anyone might have seen him at the gallery, but the area was deserted. Cars passing on the street would not have a view of the gallery door because of all the cars in the parking lot. He pulled out his shirt tail and used it to wipe the door handle, then walked back to the house to call Tio Manuel,

"We have some big problems," he said when his uncle answered the phone. "Leo is gone and the guy with the gallery? The one who took Leo in? He's dead, looks like he overdosed on the pills your boss arranged for Leo."

"Oh Jesus," groaned Manuel. "Did anyone see you there? "

"No, I don't think so."

"Where would Leo go?" Manuel thought a minute. "I need to call his father. Don't do anything until I call you back. Stay away from the gallery. There's nothing that can put you there, right?"

"I wiped any prints from the door handle," Gus said. "And I never touched that bottle of pills."

Gus paced while waiting for his uncle to call. Where could Leo have gone? Did he go with Julia? But Julia was gone when he came home from work and Leo was still there. Plus, he talked like he would never go anywhere with her. As much as it hurt his pride to gloss over her disregard for his feelings, Gus sent her a text.

"Is Leo with you??"

The app showed that she had read the message but she did not respond. Gus was feeling more and more angry and humiliated. A half hour later, she sent her one-word response: "No". There was no further explanation for her disappearance. He took a few deep breaths, something he had learned to do in rehab when he needed to calm down.

And suddenly, he ceased to care. Gus had seen two dead people in a matter of days. Life could be overwhelming, he thought, and a person needed help to deal with it. When a person likes you, it gives them power over you. They can enhance your life or they can set you back. Julia had been the symbol of his dream, but she was not the dream.

As he was talking himself off the ledge, his uncle called back.

"We need to find Leo," he said. "Don't worry about the guy in the gallery. Tucker has that covered. Someone will come there this evening posing as an art lover and discover the body. He will call the police. But I need you to walk the neighborhood in case Leo is out wandering around. Tucker is on his way down and will be searching too."

Before hanging up, Manuel said "I'm sorry, Gustavo, that I involved you in this. I know how hard you have worked for your sobriety and I admire you for that. I should not have let my boss pressure me. Lo siento mucho."

"It's okay, tio. But when his dad gets here, I don't want to be part of this anymore. I saw the man he killed. He was just an ordinary working guy and didn't deserve to be blown away by a junkie loser."

"Esta bien."

Gus headed out through the north parking lot so he would not pass the gallery again. The parking lot connected to a quiet residential street and Gus walked down to where it met the Alameda Drain canal. There were a few vacant houses, one looked neglected enough to house addicts. He knocked once and opened the door. Several ragged men nodded along a wall of the empty room. Leo was not among them.

Gus walked along the canal for a bit, then turned up the next residential street.. It was very narrow, he wondered how two cars could pass without colliding. But there was no traffic going either way so apparently it was not well traveled. The houses were nicer and most had adobe walls with gates on the street. Some planted corn and bamboo to shield their houses from view, but in a friendly touch there was a Free Library box affixed to one fence pole.

Gus opened the glass door and looked over the books, ranging from volumes on mathematics to children's books. Gus looked at the cover of a paperback of William Least Heat Moon's *Blue Highways*. He had always wanted to drive around the Southwest once he saved enough for a reliable car and had worked long enough to earn a vacation. He took the book, promising himself that he would bring another one to contribute to the library. There were no books in his uncle's house, but he could get one at a thrift store.

He was glancing at the back cover while he walked up the street until he became aware of someone kneeling over some wilted tomato plants in a backyard garden up ahead. When she stood up, he saw that it was the tall girl he had once seen at the gallery. His heart was beating fast. Should he ask her if she knew where Leo was? She looked at him and nodded hello with no sign of recognition.

If she doesn't recognize me, I need to stay out of it, Gus thought. Now that I know where she is, I'll tell Tucker and he can handle it. It's his problem, anyway. He returned home and perused *Blue Highways*, waiting for Leo's dad to show up. Then he would go out and buy the newspaper for the want ads. He seriously needed to move and leave Leo and Rod and Julia and all of their bullshit behind.

Leo

Leo woke up and wondered what time it was. There were no windows in the room but there seemed to be some light out in the hall. He got up and held onto the wall for a few beats before making his way to the bathroom. Rod appeared to be asleep on the futon. He wanted to borrow Rod's phone to call his father. He didn't expect to like whatever "deal" his dad was cooking up but figured he should find out who knew what. If Paloma would come with him, he would take Rod's car and all that money in the drawer and head for Mexico, Puerto Penasco was not too far, a seaside town where they could live in anonymity right on the beach. Juarez was much closer, but it was too unpredictable and Paloma would be a target for the purveyors of the local sex trade. He was going to take her away from all that, he thought. He would be heroic for one time in his life.

He noticed Rod's car keys on the desk, right next to his phone. He didn't know where to find the car but it couldn't be far away. He could walk all of Old Town after it got dark. Paloma would be coming back soon with more drugs. She probably knew where the car was but he couldn't ask because he already told her he had a car. Not too smart, Leo, he thought. Strung out or not, you have to be cool. He suspected he was being groomed as a soldier in whatever drug gang was using the gallery to launder its proceeds.

Figuring he'd wake Rod to ask about the phone, he shook his shoulder. His arm flopped in a strange way and Leo leaned in to look at his face. He definitely looked dead, probably from those pills that had been meant for him. Either way, Leo was not going to be involved. He went into the bedroom, picked up Rod's backpack and emptied the contents onto the bed. He took the backpack to the desk and again pried the drawer open, With shaking hands he stuffed all of the cash into the backpack. He grabbed the backpack, keys and phone and unlocked the door. He did not lock it behind him.

Leo huddled under the stairs to the blockhouse where he had spent the first hours of this nightmare. When Paloma arrived, he would be able to warn her and convince her to come with him. He needed what she was bringing. Once they got to Puerto Penasco, he would make some connections to tide him over until he could figure out what to do next.

As he waited, Leo saw Gus coming down the sidewalk towards his house. Leo crouched down further beneath the stairs. Gus went into his house briefly, then crossed to the gallery. He knocked, then finding the door unlocked, entered. Five minutes later he emerged, visibly upset, and went back into his house. Then it was quiet: no sirens or any sign that Gus had notified the police. Of course he would call his uncle and his uncle would call Leo's dad. Just a matter of time before he showed up. C'mon Paloma, he thought, get it in gear.

As if on cue, she turned onto the street. He walked as steadily as he could manage to meet her halfway.

"You don't want to go there," he said. "That Rod guy is dead. I think there was something else in those Oxys, or maybe he just took way too many. Anyway, he's dead. We should not be around when somebody finds him and calls the cops."

Paloma didn't seem surprised. She had spent too much time around junkies and pill heads lately to believe they all would survive their addictions. She beckoned for Leo to follow her down Hollywood Street, from where she had come.

"I can't bring you in," said Paloma. "You would have to be approved first."

She handed him a bag that contained what he needed to stay level for a while.

"Do you have somewhere to go?"

"I have money," he said. "I will check into that motel on Central. Find me there when you can."

She shook her head. "No, I can't go there. Come look for me tomorrow in the little garden in back of the house," she said.

She buzzed the call box at the gate. Leo was already moving away when the gates swung open and he saw a red Fiat Spyder parked along the wall. The license matched the one on Rod's key fob. He was hoping to find the car parked on the street somewhere, this would be trickier especially with the big dog he saw snarling under the portal. But he was sure that

Paloma would help him. She seemed to need rescuing and he was just the man for the job. Nothing like a backpack full of money and the keys to a hot car to make a loser feel like a jackpot winner.

Fortuna

Storm clouds were gathering again as she made her way back up the stairs to her balcony shelter. She tapped lightly on Milly's door and heard her cane clicking across the wood floors. Milly greeted her with a friendly smile, but Fortuna was quiet and preoccupied. Thanking Milly for her help, she walked to the balcony, unconscious of the tall bookcases she had noticed the day before. She had intended to ask Milly where she got so many books and hoped that she might be invited to borrow one. But the news about Billy had driven thoughts of books from her mind.

The rain started in earnest, and the heat of the day vanished. She pulled a light sweater from her suitcase and felt for the gun tied up in a shawl, still there. She sat on her pile of bedding and watched the rain.

Looking over the balcony rail to the tree where she had once tried to find shelter, she saw the long, black car drive through the gates and pull into the driveway of the big house on the other side of the crumbling adobe wall. It looked like the one the girl had been riding in the first day Fortuna saw her. That was also the first day she heard that song about Old Town Road that she had been thinking about. The car sat in the driveway until the rain stopped. Then the tall, heavyset man emerged from the back seat and went into the house.

Suddenly hungry, she rifled through her suitcase and found the half-finished box of crackers, As she was eating them, she heard a car pull up to the gallery door downstairs. Someone got out and went inside, If she stood up, she could have seen who it was, but she was tired. Less than ten minutes later, she heard the scream of sirens coming down Rio Grande and a line of cop cars pulled into the parking lot. There was shouting and doors slamming and a jumble of men's voices under the portal beneath her, but she couldn't make out their conversation. She listened hard, and eventually caught the words "medical examiner."

Her heart lurched. It must be that boy she saw entering the gallery a few days ago. She felt herself getting upset again. That boy had no business associating with that sleazy art dealer, she knew it then and now he was dead.

Milly opened the balcony door.

"I don't know what's happening downstairs and I can't go down there. I'll see what the neighbors know."

Fortuna nodded sadly, convinced that she knew what they would find. First Billy, she thought, and now this beautiful young man who reminded her so much of him. Later, Milly returned with a bowl of green chile stew and what little she had been able to learn.

"A man is dead down there and it looks like a drug overdose," she said.

"A young man?" asked Fortuna

"I don't know. Do you think it's someone you know?"

Fortuna shook her head.

"If I hear any more, I'll let you know."

Fortuna was hungry but felt too upset to eat. The devil was winning, everywhere. She knew she herself was undeserving, but these young people like her Billy, the boy from the river, and the dark-skinned girl who she had trailed to the house on Old Town Road, they should not be prey for evil men. She felt the hopeful attitude fade inside of her. What was the point of trying?

She unzipped her suitcase and felt for the gun. She unwrapped the shirt and glancing at the balcony door in case Milly was inside, she took the gun and shoved it between the cushions and sheets. She had no plan, but knowing that such an amoral man was living so close made her feel the need for protection. She stayed awake for a long time, listening for any activity below and watching the big house across the way. The big black car was still in the parking lot. Eventually she dozed off and when her aching neck woke her at dawn, the car was gone. She watched the sky turn pink to the west and tried to rally her flagging spirits. She couldn't summon the energy required to walk downtown and find a public telephone to call her daughter-in-law. When Milly came to the balcony door with a cup of coffee, she asked if she might borrow her phone.

"I did so much walking yesterday," she said. "But I need to check on my grandson up north. He's been having some problems."

"Of course." Milly handed Fortuna her phone and went back into the apartment to give her privacy. Fortuna's hand was shaking so bad that she misdialed and had to start over several times. Finally, her son picked up the phone.

"It's me," she said. "Can I talk to Olivia?"

"Sorry, she's not available," he said. "Billy's in trouble, big trouble." Fortuna could hear Olivia crying in the background. She felt her heart beating fast.

"Que paso?" she asked, wondering if she really wanted to know. Clearly it was something devastating; Olivia had always been the most hopeful about Billy's prospects for recovery and a normal life.

"He and some friends tried to rob a construction company in Espanola. A security guard was shot trying to stop them. He's in the hospital but he might not make it. Either way, Billy's going to prison."

"Where is he now? Can he get bail?" Fortuna knew she couldn't raise that much money, but maybe someone else would, although she couldn't think of anyone.

"They took him to the Rio Arriba County jail in Tierra Amarilla," her son said. "He'll get a public defender and will be arraigned next week. But the guard who was shot is a Sikh who was not carrying a gun so they can't claim self-defense. Billy's going away."

She hung up and left the phone on the dresser and went back to the balcony. She tried to take deep breaths to soothe herself, but she was overcome by a feeling of utter hopelessness. She had done all she could for the boy but couldn't save him from himself and the danger that lurked everywhere where poverty and undereducation led so many young men to a life of crime. Can't nobody tell me nothing.

She knocked and entered the apartment. Milly was sitting on the couch reading a book.

"I need to go out," Fortuna said. "I need to walk so I can think."

Milly looked concerned but nodded her head. Fortuna walked to the Plaza. A group of women in shorts were congregated in front of one of the tourist shops, talking and laughing, Fortuna hated them. How dare they be acting so foolish when Fortuna's life had been turned upside down?

She pushed past them without apology. She walked the perimeter of the Plaza, seeing nothing, trying unsuccessfully to calm herself. She found a vacant bench and sat down but was soon approached by a man selling balloons he fashioned into animals. He stopped in front of her and began twisting balloons together, presumably for her entertainment.

"Why is he looking at me? I can't think with him squeaking those pinche balloons."

She rose abruptly and crossed the street to the church and went inside. For a time, she sat alone near the back, her mind darting here and there, trying to wind back time and reveal a different fate for her grandson. Tears began to roll down her cheeks and she did not wipe them away. A single phone call had taken away her reason to live.

She became aware that she was not alone. A woman in a headscarf made her way slowly down the aisle and stopped next to Fortuna.

"Can I pray with you?"

Fortuna felt her anger rise. She was trying to think, not pray. She stood up and faced the woman, who shrank back when she saw Fortuna's face.

"I prayed again and again for my grandson and now he's going to prison. If God exists, he doesn't listen to me. Go find someone else to pray with."

She walked quickly to the heavy wood door and flung it open. She didn't close it, to show her disrespect. These encounters had exhausted her and she slowly headed back to Milly's balcony.

For hours, she sat on her cushions and blankets, watching flights of birds wheeling in unison before settling back on a telephone line. The sun was hot. The monsoons appeared to be over and soon she would have no reason to sleep on Milly's balcony. She would have to decide where to go now.

Gus

Tucker Sloan was not happy.

"What the hell happened here?" he demanded the minute Gus opened the door. "I was making arrangements to take care of this mess and now Leo's disappeared? How is this possible?"

Like most rich men, he couldn't handle it when his plans were thwarted, Gus thought. He had met Tucker while accompanying his uncle on his rounds delivering firewood to his clients. The richer the client, the more fireplaces would need to be stocked. Sloan would inspect the wood and complain if it felt the quality was not up to his standards. Gus always considered him just another rich Santa Fe asshole.

"I'm sorry," he said. "Tony, the guy you hired to bring Leo some pills, took off after his girlfriend crashed his car. I'm in recovery and I can't be around drugs so Leo was crashing at the gallery. The dead guy was supposed to be keeping an eye on him, but it looks like he was dipping into his supply instead."

"What do you mean?"

"The bottle of pills Tony brought for Leo were on a table next to the gallery guy's body," Gus said. "Either he took too many or they're laced with something else. The newspapers say street drugs are full of Fentanyl."

"But if the drugs are still in the gallery, how is Leo managing his withdrawal? It's only been a couple of days. He's gonna still be sick."

Gus considered whether he should tell Tucker about the tall girl and the house on Hollywood. He didn't want to bring trouble down on her, but it was the only clue he had to Leo's whereabouts. It had gotten late and he wasn't feeling good about approaching this forbidding house in the dark. Tucker took him off the hook by announcing that he would go driving around the UNM campus with Leo's picture to see if he could pick up any clues to his whereabouts. Leo still knew people on campus, even though he was considerably older that the average student.

"Okay," he said. "I'll stay here in case he comes back."

"He won't," Tucker said. "There's a dead guy over there and he knows it. Besides, the cops will be here soon, so I'd advise you to stay inside and don't offer any information. Is there anyone else who knew that Leo was staying there?"

Again, Gus thought about the girl, but didn't want to get roped into going to the Hollywood house in the dark. If Tucker had no luck, he would suggest gong there in the morning before work. He could say he hadn't been sure it was the same girl until he saw her on the street. Ten minutes after Tucker left, he heard police sirens coming up Rio Grande and through his windows could see the red lights flashing as the cars turned into the driveway between his house and the gallery. He did as Tucker said and didn't go outside. He put on some headphones so he could pretend not to have notice the activity outside. He could see that the red-haired masseuse whose shop was next door to the gallery was out under the portal watching the officers, and eventually the medical examiner, come and go.

There was a knock on his door and he opened it to a brown-skinned officer. He looked young,

"Sorry to bother you, bro, but did you know the guy who worked in the gallery over there?"

"I've seen him around," Gus said. "Can't say I know him. What's going on?"

"Somebody OD'd in the gallery. Have you seen anyone else go in there?

"No, but I work all day," Gus said. "And when I come home I'm beat and just want to watch tv. I don't know much about what happens around here,"

The cop pulled up a picture on his phone and showed it to Gus.

"This the guy you saw working in the gallery?"

He had taken a picture of Ron's swollen, discolored face. Gus glanced at it, then closed his eyes.

"Yes, I think so. It's kind of hard to tell."

The cop thanked him and Gus closed the door. How had he gotten involved in something so sordid? He was so determined to stay on the good foot and live a clean life yet here he was, covering for drug dealers and murderers. And for what? Julia was gone and most probably wouldn't come back. And he would not take her back in any case. It would hurt for a while, he knew, the death of his dream. But he could find a new one. But first he would have to extricate himself from the morass of evil in which he found himself.

He went to the storeroom and got the boxes he used to bring his clothes and video games to Albuquerque after leaving rehab. He hoped his uncle would understand, but he had to get away from here. After he packed his possessions, he unlocked the door for Tucker and wrote him a note: I have to work at nine. But at 8:30 I will take you to someone who may know something. Gus

He left the note on the table and went to bed. The red lights from the cop cars were still flashing outside but his mind had calmed now that he had an exit strategy. He slept soundly. In the morning, he made as much noise as possible getting ready for work. He saw that Tucker had slept on the couch with the blankets Gus had left for him. He didn't stir, but for Gus it was now or never.

"Hey Mr. Sloan, if you want to come with me now I can show you a house where I have seen a friend of Leo's," he said, "But I have to go to work and won't get a break until one or two. So we'd better do this now."

Tucker apparently wasn't a morning person and said nothing, but he sat up and put on his shoes. He ran his fingers through his hair to tame it a bit and looked around the kitchen.

"No coffee?" he growled.

"I have coffee at the diner, sorry."

The sky was still rosy in the west although the sun had been up for hours. Maybe it meant the monsoons were over, Gus thought. There had already been enough rain, He and Tucker walked down Hollywood and stopped at the black iron gate. Tucker pressed the intercom buzzer. There was no answer, so he buzzed again, repeatedly. Finally, a voice crackled through.

"Quien es?"

"He wants to know who you are," Gus said.

"Never mind that," said Tucker. "I'm looking for my son, Leo, Is he here?"

"De que? No conosco Leo."

"Una chica...flaca...bella. Estaba con ella," Gus said,

"No, no, aqui no." After that, there was no response, no matter how much Tucker buzzed the intercom. The conversation, such as it was, was over.

"I have to go to work," Gus said. "Please lock the front door on your way out, you can do it from inside. Good luck but I don't think I can help you anymore."

He turned and walked toward the diner; he did not look back to see what Tucker would do. On his lunch break, he would get a newspaper and find a new furnished apartment. He could afford a cab to take his boxes there. When he got to the diner, Lorena seemed pleased to see him and he stopped and gave her his most charming smile.

"Good morning, you look so nice today."

The girl was clearly not expecting such interest; Gus had a reputation for being remote and businesslike.

"Good morning," she replied.

What a difference a day makes. He decided to ask that girl to dinner and the movies. Time to move on.

Juan

Juan had been feeling down lately. He thought that Rod might be his replacement: someone who could handle simple administrative tasks and ride herd on the drivers. If he could find a suitable replacement, maybe the boss would let him go back up north.

But Rod obviously had no ambition, at least not in that business. He liked the money, but Juan could tell he was bored and would leave at the first opportunity. That was the reason he kept Rod's car over at the Hollywood house.

Juan felt he had proved his loyalty over the months since he had become ensnared in the drug business. He didn't go out and drink in the bars and run his mouth and he had no weakness for the kinds of girls he saw at the house. He had grown fond of Paloma since she had started coming around, but it was understood that she belonged to Antonio and no one questioned that. But he could also see that she shared his dream to escape. She seemed so much more alive when Antonio was gone, as he was with increasing frequency.

"Haven't seen the boss around lately," he said.

"Probably means the operation will be moving soon," said one of the young men who lived at the house. "There's business in every city and it don't pay to stay in one place too long."

Albuquerque was conveniently located for transport at the intersection of two major interstates, but it was a small enough city that sooner or later the cops would start to notice and trail the drivers.

Allowing Leo to stay in the gallery was another attempt to find a replacement for himself. If Rod would handle the money, at least the kid could replace one of the drivers who had recently been deported back to Mexico. Leo didn't seem to have any other skills but he was the most desirable kind of employee for the business: he was addicted to their product and had no intention of stopping, So he would be easy to pay and easy to keep.

Lately he had been noticing that Leo had eyes for Paloma. But Leo was so obviously a fuck up that Juan was afraid that if those two tried to escape, Antonio would kill them both without a second thought. Paloma had not been able to hide her sadness and Antonio had grown bored with her. Juan wished that he could help her, but had to concentrate on helping himself. If he could just get out of this mess, he would go back to Pojoaque and try to get a computing job at Los Alamos. They were always trying to increase their minority hires so maybe they wouldn't be so concerned about his departure from INTEL. If he could just take Paloma with him and leave Leo to work with the gang, that would be perfect.

Leo

Leo had two problems: he needed another fix and he needed to find a way to get Rod's car out of the parking lot with its locked gate. Paloma seemed to be the solution to both but how to get rid of her after getting her help? He had decided that she was too repressed to be an amusing companion. She looked hot, but she gave off a chilly vibe. So he needed to enlist her help in liberating the car, but he also needed more drugs until he could sort himself out. He had plenty of money to pay for the drugs but that would raise suspicion. Maybe he could claim to have a new territory for the Hollywood street crew. But the car was the bigger problem.

Leo shoved a couple of fifty dollar bills in his pocket and slung his backpack over his shoulder. He walked down the arroyo behind the motel until he got to the far end of Hollywood and then walked east. When he got to the dying garden behind the house, he stopped and scouted the area for a place where he could wait for Paloma to make an appearance. There was a trio of raggedy trees across the street from the garden that would shield him from view. The ground was elevated enough that he could also observe the gate, in case anyone arrived or left.

Since Rod was dead, the car would not be reported stolen so he could drive it to Mexico. He could drop Paloma off somewhere, give her some money for her silence. She hadn't seemed too fond of Rod so he didn't expect she would mind that he took his car. She would not want to be found by the drug dealers who lived in the house but he could take her to one of the Pueblos on his way west. She would be safe there.

But the first thing he needed was another good hit to get started and a couple more for the road. His father had friends in Mexico. He'd make the old man feel guilty for hooking him up with lethal street drugs and not coming to get him sooner. He could lay low in Mexico until everyone had forgotten about the man with the bike.

Late in the afternoon as he was dreaming of his Mexican idyll, Paloma appeared in the garden across the street, She was wearing a simple shift dress and huaraches and carried a large watering can. She looked around to see if anyone was coming down the street, then beckoned to Leo.

"What will you do now?" she asked, "If I help you take the car, you will have to take me with you. They will make me disappear."

"I will take you with me," Leo said, "but I need another shot and some for the road. Just until I can get back in touch with my guys." He pulled the two fifty dollar bills from his pocket and handed them to Paloma.

"I can pay," he said. "So if you can buy it, go ahead."

She looked at the money in her hand for a minute. There was no question of buying heroin from Juan or any of the other guys who lived in the house, delivering drugs to customers in prearranged parking lots where they would not be easily spotted. But a hundred dollars would buy her a bus ticket to Laguna Pueblo. The boss, who insisted that she call him Papa, would not be able to track her down once she was inside the Pueblo. She would have to take some drugs from the shelf in the kitchen, then wait for an opportunity to open the gate for Leo.

"Can you climb this fence?" she asked. "You can wait along the north side of the house so you can see the gate open, then get to the car. Once you are out the gate, you can wait for me by the garden." The chain link fence around the garden was only eight feet tall, and Leo got over easily. Together, they crept along the side of the house, crouching in order to throw no shadows on the ground. As they were approaching the corner, the gate swung open and the black Escalade drove in. The big man in the black suit and sunglasses emerged from the backseat. Through the window, he handed the driver a bill.

"There's a car wash at the end of Rio Grande," he said. "Go take care of that, then come back for me."

The black car exited the gate, which closed behind it. The big man went into the house.

Leo looked at Paloma, who had turned pale.

"I didn't expect him to come here so early," she said. "This might be a little harder but maybe I can make a distraction somewhere. Just be watching and be ready. The minute you see the gate start to open, run for the car. We won't have much time to make it out."

Leo nodded and felt for the car keys in his pocket. He just hoped it all wouldn't take too long. He wanted out of here NOW. Paloma went back to the garden and found a few tomatoes that weren't too green. She took the tomatoes and the watering can and went into the house.

Less than five minutes later, he saw the gate begin to swing open and saw Paloma run out the door carrying a paper sack. They both ran for the car as the door behind Paloma opened again. There was an enraged howl of anger and curses, followed by a shot. Leo was already steering the car out the driveway when Paloma yanked open the passenger door and threw herself in. One leg still outside the door scraped against the side of the stone gate as they barely slid through, turned left and headed for Rio Grande.

J

Juan

Juan was getting dressed upstairs when he heard Antonio yelling and then the shot. He ran outside and saw the big man lying face down in the dirt. There was blood streaming from somewhere. Juan and Andres, the driver, gently rolled him over. He was unconscious but breathing. The boys were gathered around.

"Que paso?"

"Somebody stole that Anglo dude's car, and it looked like he stole Paloma too."

"Never mind that," Juan said. "We need to get the boss out of here before someone reports the shot and the police show up."

"Quien le mato?"

"He's not dead," Juan said. "But we can't take him to a hospital… too many questions. Help me get him into the car. Andres, take him to El Paso, he has a private doctor there. I'll find you the address. The rest of you, help me clear out the house. Take all the drugs and money and all your personal stuff in case someone tries to track you down."

Andres helped Juan lift Antonio into the car. Antonio groaned but didn't open his eyes. The bullet had gone straight through his back and smashed a rib in its exit. Juan took off his shirt and ripped it into strips, which he tied around Antonio as tightly as he dared. As soon as he finished, he gestured to Andres to go out the open gate. Not much point in closing it anymore.

The young men were coming out of the house with large, black garbage bags tied up at the top. The began tossing the bags into the trucks and other vehicles.

"It's clean!" said the last one out. He unchained the dog and opened the back of one of the trucks. The dog jumped in. All the vehicles exited the yard one by one and turned right onto Hollywood to avoid a big street.

They all knew how to get out of town while avoiding high observation areas.

Juan watched them go, then went back into the house to get his backpack and to make sure there was nothing there that could tie him to being there. There were a few odds and ends he took—scraps of paper with numbers, probably nothing that made sense but maybe someone's handwriting would be important. He didn't dare take the time to wipe fingerprints, but hoped for the usual ineptitude from the local cops.

He walked out of the house without closing the door, then out the open gate. He needed to take care of the house on Old Town Road. When he arrived there, it looked locked up tight, but Juan had a key for emergencies. He unlocked the gate and entered the house. He wandered from room to room, looking for anything that might be incriminating to him but he found nothing. Not an important cog in the machine I guess, he thought.

But in the last bedroom he checked, he found Paloma's clothes and schoolbooks. He found a gym bag in a closet and put all her things inside. Maybe she was being kidnapped by the kid who stole the car, but maybe she was just trying to get free. Maybe she would still find some use for those schoolbooks, Juan took his backpack and the gym bag and walked out the back door. He jumped a low wall and headed for the Plaza. He left the doors and the gate open.

Fortuna

She lost track of time, sitting on the floor of the balcony watching the sky and wishing she could turn the clock back to when Billy was a happy toddler who loved animals and books. He had always been special to her: the first grandchild and the one who seemed most like her. They would take long walks and say hello to all the horses and cows they met. In their village, animals often wandered free but never ran away and Billy knew most of them by name when he was three years old.

He also liked to sit with her, surrounded by children's books that she would read one by one. One of her Christmas gifts to him that year was *Black Beauty.* He loved it and slept with it under his pillow for weeks. But as he grew older, Billy was less interested in books or his grandmother, for that matter. He became part of a gang of boys who rode the same bus down to school in the Valley and because he lacked a strong father figure, he was easily persuaded to participate in pranks that became more serious as the boys got bolder and required more danger to feel grownup and macho like their brothers and older cousins. That was when she lost him, Fortuna decided. If she could have taken him away from that place before he started school, she might have succeeded in guiding him towards a better future. But since that time, it had always been too late.

Later in the afternoon, the sun's rays began to hit the balcony and she moved back to where it was still in shadow. She sat up straight so she could see through the wooden slats of the balcony railing and noticed two figures at the far end of the house across the vacant lot. As she squinted in the sun, she could see that one was the dark girl who she had seen going into the gallery. As the pair inched along the side of the house, her heart leapt into her throat when she saw that it was the young boy who reminded her of Billy. He was not the overdose victim! It must have been the other one who died. She felt a wave of relief and gratitude that this boy, at least, was okay. She wished there was something more she could do for him.

"Ofelia, I want to help him. And her too. But what can I do?"

As she watched the pair talking at the corner of the house, the gate swung open and the shiny black car she had seen so many times before drove in. The girl and the boy retreated along the side of the house until they vanished around the corner. Fortuna saw the big man get out and stand beside the car, speaking to the driver who rolled up his window and drove out again. The big man went into the house. The gate closed. A few minutes later, the dark girl came around the house alone and walked slowly along the portal. When she reached the door, she hesitated, then went inside.

Where did the boy go? Why didn't he go into the house with the girl? She stood up to see if she could see around the corner of the house from this vantage point but she could not. The house, indeed the entire neighborhood, was still. The dog was sleeping under the portal and seemed to be tied. It had not approached the man or the girl when they entered the yard.

She watched as the gate swung open again and then everything happened so fast she would find it hard to reconstruct the events, even much later. The boy came around the house at a run and headed for a small red car parked at the corner of the lot. The girl ran from the house carrying a paper bag and headed for the same car. But the big man was just steps behind her, and the sun glinted off a large carving knife in his hand.

"Puta!" screamed the man. "Ahora te va a matar."

The scene did not seem real, it was more like a dream and Fortuna moved like a sleepwalker. But she found the gun in her good hand. She leaned the barrel on the top of the balcony rail like her father had taught her, aimed and fired. The man fell as the boy drove the car towards the gate that was beginning to close. The girl barely jumped in the passenger seat before the car squeezed out the gate.

Fortuna sat back down on the balcony floor where she could not be seen. Men poured out of the house and ran to the man lying in the dirt. One started up a pickup truck and after a few minutes some of the others lifted the wounded man into the back of the truck. The gate opened again and the truck sped away. This time, the gate did not close. The men went back into the house and came out hauling heavy garbage bags that they threw into the vehicles that remained in the yard. They unchained the dog and loaded it into the back of an SUV and one by one the cars exited the driveway. The gate did not close and silence fell again.

Fortuna was stunned that no one seemed to be looking for the shooter. Although Milly was too hard of hearing to have registered the noise as a gunshot, surely someone else in the neighborhood would have recognized the sound. But there was no body anymore and no police cars came. One of the cars that left the house drove into the gallery parking spot and went inside. She heard doors slamming and furniture being pushed around. The man came out onto the breezeway right below where Fortuna was sitting and made a call.

"The money's gone," he barked into the phone. "That pinche jodido took the money and the car."

She listened as he received his instructions.

"There's nothing else in there that could be tied to us. I'll see you tonight in Las Cruces."

He got into his car and left Fortuna wondering if she had dreamed it all. Had she killed him? If so, she was okay with that. She didn't believe that God would punish the big man and somebody needed to. But she needed to leave Milly's balcony, in case someone had seen something.

She wrapped the gun in the flannel shirt and shoved it to the bottom of her suitcase. She packed up her few belongings and folded and stacked the bedding. She put on her hat and went inside to say goodbye to her benefactor. Milly insisted that she sit down and eat another bowl of green chile stew.

"Are you sure you don't want to stay another night?" Milly asked. "It will be dark soon."

"No thank you, "said Fortuna. "Now that the rains are over, I can manage."

"Can I help you find another place to stay? Or a job?"

"I can go back to the shelter now," Fortuna said. After they ate, Milly brushed aside Fortuna's offers to help with the dishes.

"It's a long walk to the shelter from here," Milly said, pressing a dollar bill into Fortuna's hand. "Take the bus, please. And would you like to take one of my books? I know you like to read and I have so many."

Fortuna scanned the shelves and settled on a slim volume of poetry by and for women. She held it up shyly, and Milly smiled her approval.

Fortuna bumped her suitcase down the stairs and headed across the street towards Old Town Road. She needed to see what might have happened to the man she shot. When she reached Tiguex Park, she sat under the same tree where she had waited for the girl the day before. But the house was dark and the gate was wide open. There were no cars in the driveway. Like the house on Hollywood Street, it had been abandoned. Fortuna considered checking the doors in case one was open. It might be a good place to stay the night. But what if one of the men came back? No, it was a warm night with the moon shining down. She would go back to her favorite spot on the bridge. The boy was gone, hopefully far away. She didn't have to worry about identifying him. She stood up, leaning on her suitcase, and headed for Central Avenue and the river,

Leo

The Fiat barely made it through the gate and Leo was so focused on getting away that he didn't look back to see where the gunshot had come from. He assumed that it was aimed at him or at Paloma, but there was no blood and neither of them seemed to be hurt. He tore around the corner onto Rio Grande and, seeing that the light at the intersection was about to change, he floored it and careened onto Central, fishtailing and barely missing a collision with a city bus. But a cop car was among the traffic stopped at the light and before the Fiat reached the BioPark, Leo could hear the siren.

"Goddamn it," he yelled at Paloma. "What's a cop doing right there? I don't believe this."

He drove to the parking area at the far side of the Park and steered down a pedestrian path leading to the river where he rode the bike days before. Darkness was falling and the paths were deserted. Leo cut the engine and the lights and coasted underneath the bridge. It was littered with garbage and covered with graffiti but they were hidden from pursuers in cars.

"I'm going to need another car, and I can't take you along. Sorry, but this is the end of the line for us," Leo said.

He grabbed the backpack and took out another fifty dollar bill and handed it to her. He would take the rest—the drugs and the money— across the river where he would retrieve the gun he had hidden in the hollow tree a few days earlier.

He didn't look back but plunged into the water near where he had crossed previously. But the rains had done their work and the river was flowing higher. After his first few steps, the water swept him off his feet and pulled him under. He lost his hold on the backpack, which floated away. Leo's head came up once downstream and he was coughing up river water when something under the water caught and pulled hm under. He did not come up again. Paloma took the money he left in her hand, and ran back up the path towards the street. She crossed and waited for the bus that would take her downtown. She would catch a bus back to Pojoaque, see about finishing school and put the Albuquerque nightmare behind her.

Fortuna

When she arrived back at her bench on the bridge, there was a warm breeze blowing through the cottonwoods along the river bank. Fortuna breathed in the scents of the river and the bosque, happy to be back where she had felt most at home in Albuquerque. She spread a sweater out on the concrete across from the bench, intending to stay all night in this familiar place. The events of the last few days seemed more than ever like a dream.

"Did I really shoot someone, Ofelia? I'm not sorry, not really. Whether he is alive or dead, he was a bad man who wanted to harm the jovenes. I helped them to escape to a better place, a better life."

The moon was so bright she was able to read the last pages of *The Great Gatsby* and was shocked that the man whose wife had been run down killed Gatsby, who was not driving the car. She had grown fond of Jay Gatsby, pitied him and would have preferred to see any of the other characters killed. Momentarily, she wondered if the man she shot might have had children, a mother he cherished. But she saw the knife. This was not the same. She agreed with Wilson, Gatsby's killer, that the wicked must be punished in life.

She began to imagine a different future for herself.

"I can use my disability checks to fix my teeth. I have all these gaps in my mouth because when I was young, there was never money for a dentist. Tu recuerdas abuela, if you had a toothache, daddy pulled it out with a string tied to the handle of a door that he slammed shut."

Now that Billy could no longer benefit from her help, she could spend the money however she pleased. She was probably too old for a job, but maybe she could do that too. There were Help Wanted signs at many of the Old Town businesses. If she had a job, she could get an apartment. Milly would probably help her with job applications and give her a letter of reference. She drifted off to sleep on these dreams.

When she awoke it was dawn and the sky to the west had turned from gray to pink then orange. There was some activity downriver by Bridge St. Police cars were stopped on that bridge, Fortuna could see their lights flashing from her post upriver. There were two boats in the water and men with big hooks seemed to be retrieving something floating near the bridge abutment. A few hours later, a tow truck drove noisily down the footpath to the bosque visible from the bridge. But when it returned, towing the red Fiat from under the bridge, Fortuna was lost in her new poetry book and the beautiful words wiped her world clean of the ugliness around her. An extraordinary gift for hope. Jay Gatsby had it and so did she. But there was nowhere for Gatsby to go but down. And Fortuna could smell and taste her new life arriving on the warm air and the timeless flow of the river.

Readers Guide

1. Fortuna is an elderly and injured woman living on the streets of Albuquerque, where she knows no one. Is she very brave or very foolish?

2. Leo is a grown man who looks like a boy. How does this affect how people react to him?

3. Leo resembles Fortuna's grandson Billy. How does this impact the trajectory of the story?

4. Gus is building his future around Julia, who he doesn't really know well. What are the clues he is ignoring?

5. Gus is trying to maintain sobriety while hosting drunks and drug addicts at his uncle's house. Is he setting himself up for failure?

6. Rod has all the ingredients for success but his life story is failure after failure. When and why does this pattern begin?

7. Juan is a smart guy but not a good judge of people. How might he have avoided becoming involved with a criminal gang?

8. After she is assaulted by the drug lord, Paloma does not try to escape. In her place, what would you do?

9. Milly invites a stranger to sleep on her balcony. Was that unwise? Would you do it?

10. Old Town is a historic place that sits next to a neighborhood filled with all the ills of the modern age. Why do you think this is and how do they relate to each other?

Printed in the USA
CPSIA information can be obtained
at www.ICGtesting.com
LVHW031123200624
783570LV00038B/147

Praise for *Hechizo, Exile Home, That Train Again, A Map of the Winds*, and Mark Statman

The spell of Mark Statman's magical, marvelously absorbing *Hechizo* begins with Furies and ends in Love. The poems casual yet perfectly poised short lines engender a sense of unbreakable continuity, until there's "nothing/left but ash and/unmoving angelic their/feathered wings" as they bring all opposites together "when change/and the same are/the same." They are an endless source of delight.

—John Koethe

The poems in Statman's beautiful new book *Hechizo* occupy the thin place between life and death, dream and waking, love and loss. His words cast a spell on the reader; one can hear the music in each line—as if there were a voice emanating from the page. In his work, the Mexican landscape is pulsating with life, but so are the recently and long dead, as well as vibrant memories of life and people left behind. ...to read this book is to remember what it feels like to be fully alive.

—Joanna Fuhrman

A *hechizo* is, for good or ill, a spell, a kind of magic cast into or from life's uncertainties, an act of language, eliciting both the furies of a corrupt world and the redemptions of love, poetry in its earliest and most enduring form. Mark Statman's *Hechizo* draws on both types of spells with an urgent lyricism , at once quick-moving and inclusive. There is a unique capacity here for engaging the furies of the social and political fully with the self, a measure of judgment and complicity, akin to the morally complex rhapsodic traditions of modern poetry in Spanish, which Statman successfully engaged with as a translator. The collection ends with a section of love poems, also called "Hechizo," redemptive but hardly certain, the prospect of love, for his parents, for two strangers sighted in the park, for himself. This is a powerful collection, personal, in the best, most richly evolved sense.

—Michael Anania

Como todo conocedor de su oficio, el poeta Mark Statman sabe que la estructura que sostiene al mundo es el lenguaje, sabe que sólo así podemos conocerlo, admirarlo, actuar en él. Como todo conocedor de su oficio.

Statman sabe que un poema es una acción ritual, una fórmula precisa que abre en algún grado nuestro horizonte de realidad. Eso es *Hechizo*.

—*Efraín Velasco*

Mark Statman's *Exile Home* is a love poem, a snapshot, to the poet's adopted country so fresh in the poem "Mi México". The air, the light, the poignancy of little girl with wooden bowl, & mystery of life next to another, a beloved partner, buzz with sharp grace. A contrast across the border, with family loss, but no walls, here. Power of "all the unseen… writ in glass in water clouds" join the fiesta. No ideas but in things. I want to go there too. This is a sweet and pungent sensory exile, almost a dream.

—*Anne Waldman*

Exile Home is an elegiac journey of discovery: "the room / that lights / the house" is the possibility of coming to be who you are in whatever place we find ourselves. These are poems of transition as a form of mediation and meditation. Mark Statman's short lines mark the flux of sentiment as openness to what's next. "can you believe / we live like this"? Only time tells.

—*Charles Bernstein*

Mark Statman's fiercely elegiac book begins with the long poem, "Green Side Up," dedicated to his father. Written in lower case with no punctuation, it provides quick flashes of family memory and the present reality of grief. The reader is utterly absorbed and lifted: "on the phone / you say it's/ another DIP / day in paradise / waking early enough / there were no / sounds of morning / only birdsong breeze / the meaning of paradise / that first moment / alone and taking in / coffee and sunlight." This is realism in the most beautiful sense. We are taken to the living moment as it passes. Italo Calvino wrote of "the moral values invested in the most tenuous traces." It's in "the intensity of minor acts" (John Ashbery) that we are folded into the cloak of truth: "we did this / we did this / it happened / before we thought it." It was "a voice made for radio": "*Al Statman here / good morning.*"

—*Paul Hoover*

At his best, Mark Statman whimsically seduces us to plug what large emptiness we carry into the day. Such a playfulness of spirit and sound, not yet outlawed in these parts, lifts us toward some unforeseen feeling or study of human life that would have eluded us, were it not for his sparse and controlled lines. Here is an eclectic imagination that redeems the conventional exploits of language and all the dead zones around us. *Exile Home* consecrates Statman's forever voice.

—Major Jackson

Sieve-like and shifty language with more directness and clarity than obfuscation and obtuseness. The father poem of *Exile Home*, "Green Side Up," is a triumph of courage and poetry and love. From it the manuscript opens like a flower of multiple petals. I am enthralled by a seeming innocence and a creeping wisdom, which, rather than distort the innocence, strengthens it. After all, we have the choice to see the world as unconcerned about our troubles in it. It is the world, not a bark on which we float toward happiness. An assertion of the will to see hope as language-driven, music-clad. Mr. Yeats and his wind-up birds. There are many drowsy emperors out there.

—Pablo Medina

To date, in spite of an incredibly productive and much lauded career as a poet, Mark Statman's greatest claim to fame is his astonishing translation, with Pablo Medina, of García Lorca's *Poet in New York*. *Exile Home* changes all that.

—John Yamrus

Although the poems in Mark Statman's lovely *That Train Again* break down into sections and titles, you could almost read this book as a long, sweet poetic day of meditation; earth sky, birds, winds, wife, love, and the ways they attach themselves to the poet and, through him, to us. A good book of poetry will urge us not to miss the fine details. Here is music to slow the pulse and re-tune the ear to what is important.

—Cornelius Eady

Mark Statman's spare, candid poems speak of the ways a person moves "from fold/into blue." *That Train Again* details out daily translation of "world/into world."

--Idra Novey

Mark Statman's voice brings together historical awareness with mindful surrender for the present moments (that sometimes calls back memories from psyche's depths). Mark Statman's lines are maps of the wind that carry us into wonder and love.

—Aliki Barnstone

Sung through a register of gentle if unrelenting consciousness on the part of the poet that the present is always inexhaustibly on the move, Statman's spare, concise, searching poems channel notations of experience through the visual and aural senses.

—Anselm Berrigan

Statman's voice is a kind of spare lyricism that reminds me of the ancient Greek poets of the Anthology or the concise voicings of Antonio Machado.

—Joseph Stroud

...an admirably light touch illuminates the seriousness behind the poems...

—Tony Towle

Mark Statman delivers the tourist's wonder and distance in spare deliberate music—American's grand plain poetry descended from William Carlos Williams to James Schuyler. Statman is a head-on poet willing to risk clarity in pursuit of the marvelous we might encounter anywhere.

—William Corbett

Statman gives us language as commitment, commitment as imagination, imagination as soul-making

—Joseph Lease

It's very rare to watch the birth of a new style. It's like watching through new set of Proust's kaleidoscopes. Mark Statman has been working for years on a vision of himself and parts of the city—concentrated and bare as any poetry. It's hard to compare it to anything else.

—David Shapiro